★ MAVERICKS

Return to Whitehorn

Welcome to Whitehorn, Montana—the home of bold men and daring women. A place where rich tales of passion and adventure are unfolding under the Big Sky. Seems that this charming little town has some mighty big secrets. And everybody's talking about...

Carey Hall—Whitehorn's pediatrician. Expert at delivering small doses of the sweetest bedside manner this side of the Mississippi—enough to make men forget about pain and forget why they have steered clear of romance.

J. D. Cade—He's just about to leave Whitehorn behind—again—until he learns his sister is in desperate straits. And in order to save her, he must reveal a twenty-five-year-old secret that could destroy all the trust he's built up till now.

Jennifer McCallum—Everyone has taken an interest in this tiny tot's welfare, ever since the day she was found in a basket on the doorstep of the Kincaid ranch house. Now the adorable three-year-old is in desperate need of a bone marrow transplant. Could this child be the catalyst that sparks a romance between J.D. and Carey?

LAURIE PAIGE

A Hero's Homecoming

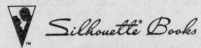

Published by Silhouette Books

America's Publisher of Contemporary Romance

Special thanks and acknowledgment to Laurie Paige
for her contribution to the Montana Mavericks series.

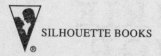 SILHOUETTE BOOKS

Recycling programs
for this product may
not exist in your area.

ISBN-13: 978-0-373-36210-3

A HERO'S HOMECOMING

Printed in U.S.A.

LAURIE PAIGE

"One of the nicest things about writing romances is researching locales, careers and ideas. In the interest of authenticity, most writers will try anything... once." Along with her writing adventures, Laurie has been a NASA engineer, a past president of the Romance Writers of America, a mother and a grandmother. She was twice a Romance Writers of America RITA® Award finalist for Best Traditional Romance and has won awards from *RT Book Reviews* for Best Silhouette Special Edition and Best Silhouette Book in addition to appearing on the *USA TODAY* bestseller list. Settled in Northern California, Laurie is looking forward to whatever experiences her next novel will bring.

One

The door of the Hip Hop Café swung open. A cowboy in a thigh-length shearling jacket strode inside on a swirl of frosty January air. The chill mingled with the laughter that flowed around Dr. Carey Hall. She pulled the cardigan draped over her shoulders closer around her.

Watching the cowboy, she noted his quick survey of the restaurant. His eyes were a startling blue in the deeply tanned face. Whatever thoughts flickered in those azure depths were sternly hidden behind a granite shield.

J. D. Cade looked like a man who'd hit the road at an early age...and the road had hit back.

While his expression showed no emotion, his face was weathered and craggy, his body lean and sinewy, like that of a lobo who lived by his wits at the edges of civilization. There was silver in his hair, although it was difficult to see among the sun-bleached strands of light and dark blond.

A man who'd been there, done that.

His restless gaze skimmed past her, paused, then returned. In the space between two heartbeats, his eyes locked with hers.

During that split second, sparks seemed to fly between them as they had the first time she'd seen him at the Kincaid ranch—the day she'd taken care of Suzanne Paxton's brother. She'd felt that tingle of electricity each time the two had met during the months since his arrival in Whitehorn, Montana. Finally his gaze moved on, and she was released from the spell he cast.

She looked around the crowded room, her heart racing a bit. Every table was filled. If she'd been alone, would he have joined her? From someplace deep inside, the answer leaped into her mind...*yes.* Just last week he'd headed straight for her, then Reed Austin had called him over to his table.

A momentary lull heightened the awareness of the outsider's presence, then conversation resumed, but at a lower pitch, as if the diners now huddled closer, wariness seeping into the earlier cheer they'd shared in the odd little restaurant.

They should be wary. An alien, dangerous and self-contained, was in their midst. The man looked as out of place among the bric-a-brac of the café as that off-breed mongrel he owned would have looked at a purebred dog show.

He crossed the café in a rangy, almost insolent, slouch and chose a stool at the counter, then ordered the dinner special. His voice drifted across the room, deep and gruff—the growl of a beast from deep in a cave. It carried an element of menace, of danger best avoided.

She sensed a slight easing of tension in the atmosphere now that the invader had settled. Or maybe she was the only one who felt on edge. It had been a hard week at the hospital. She wasn't in the mood for fun and laughter. Not tonight.

She forced herself to relax and smile. The jokes of her companions had turned risqué. Susan, the senior staff nurse in pediatrics, had recently become engaged and they were having a congratulatory dinner for her.

"You have to train them right from the start," Annie, who looked like a curly-topped version of Raggedy Ann and was loved by every child in the pediatric wing, advised. "Every time he leaves his dirty socks on the floor, sweep them into the dustpan and dump them into the trash. That teaches him real quick to put stuff in its proper place."

"Did you do that to Bill?" someone asked.

She grinned sheepishly. "For two weeks. When he ran out of socks, he bought more. When I asked him about it, he admitted he thought I washed only once a month and he didn't want to admit he didn't have enough clothes to last that long."

Carey laughed with the other women.

"But I also showed him the washing machine and

taught him how it works. Are you going to do that with Ken?" Annie demanded of the senior nurse.

Susan sighed and gazed at her ring, turning her hand so the diamond flashed. "I don't know." She sighed again. "Women are such fools."

Carey knew what was troubling Susan. They'd talked about it at lunch one day before Susan had accepted the proposal. Like Carey, the nurse was divorced. Susan's marriage had fallen apart because of another woman, Carey's because of her career. Medicine and marriage didn't mix, not in her experience.

No. It had been more than the demands of her job that had caused the failure. She'd thought she could be the emotional anchor for Jack. She'd tried to give him the stability she'd thought he'd needed. She'd learned that wasn't possible.

He'd been restless and fed up with small-town life within a year. After moving from job to job for two more years, he'd finally taken one in another state and demanded she go with him *snap!* just like that. She'd refused.

End of marriage.

She sighed. They'd been divorced for three years. At times the loneliness got to her, and she regretted the split. However, she'd gotten Sophie out of the deal. The five-year-old was the bright spot of her life, her reward for the long days of worrying about other people's children.

Her eyes went to the long, lean cowboy, who was still a stranger in spite of the months he'd been in town. He might fill the lonely hours, but she sensed he, too, wasn't a man to hang around for the long haul. She knew herself. Like moss, she wanted to grow on a stone that would stay put.

"The other nurses wanted me to ask," Annie's laughter-filled voice interrupted, "is this a want-to marriage or a have-to?"

Since Susan was well past fifty, this brought another round of giggles.

"Have to," Susan replied, undaunted by the younger nurse's teasing. Her voice dropped to confidential tones. "His mom came by last Sunday and caught us…"

"Yes?" three voices chorused.

"Making pancakes."

"Phooey," Annie said. "That's nothing."

"We weren't wearing much of anything at the time," Susan finished with a demure smile.

The group voiced a satisfied, "Aah."

"My dad would kill me if he ever found me at a man's house making pancakes, even if I wore a suit of armor," bemoaned Sara, the youngest of their staff, an eighteen-year-old records clerk fresh out of high school.

Carey cast the girl a sympathetic smile. Her thoughts shifted as the conversation again centered on the wedding. She felt death as a lurking specter at her elbow.

Jennifer McCallum was seriously ill. Baby Jennifer, as the reporters had called her when she'd been found, was an abandoned child who had turned into an heiress when it was discovered she was the illegitimate daughter of the late Jeremiah Kincaid, who had been the richest rancher in those parts. Jennifer had been adopted by a social worker named Jessica Larson, who'd married the deputy sheriff, Sterling McCallum.

Carey fought the despair that threatened to engulf her. She'd received the test results that afternoon. Jennifer, that laughing, mischievous three-year-old, had leukemia, and the chemotherapy wasn't working.

The café blurred. Carey blinked rapidly.

Glancing away from the chattering group at her table, she encountered eyes as blue as topaz. J.D. watched her with an intensity that reached right down inside her and shook something free that had been tied up for a long time.

His gaze held her. She fought it for a few seconds before giving in. She let herself drift like a piece of flotsam in a warm sea as he continued to study her. His gaze became warmer…hot…

A slow smile kicked up one corner of his mouth, as if he mocked the attraction that had sparked between them from the first minute they'd met. She trembled, but didn't—couldn't—look away.

Hunger opened like a chasm inside her. He could fill that need….

She had a sudden image of his lean body pressed over hers, filling her with his hot demands, bringing ecstasy and forgetfulness, if only for an hour or two. She wanted that.

One night of mindless bliss.

Sophie was at her first sleepover at a friend's home. No one would have to know. Dear God, she was insane.

Without breaking eye contact, he picked up his coffee mug and took a drink. His hands were slender, the fingers aristocratically long.

A cowboy would have calluses. She would feel the slight abrasion from them when he touched her in all the places that hadn't been stroked in years—

She silently gasped when she realized the direction her thoughts had taken. However, it wasn't the first time she'd had erotic daydreams about J. D. Cade.

That fact confused her. She wasn't a man-hungry woman. She'd never been boy crazy as a teenager. She didn't flirt or dress provocatively or wear makeup. Medicine had been her goal, her first love, even back then.

Tonight, she had other things to think of, important things that didn't include an interlude with a drifter who would probably move on when the next fierce storm of the year came blowing through.

Running before the wind was the term for cows that got lost in a storm. They blindly and instinctively walked in the direction the wind was blowing. Like tumbleweeds.

And men like J. D. Cade.

She was distracted when the waitress poured fresh coffee for them. She picked up the cup and took a sip, welcoming its warmth all the way to her stomach. When she looked up, J.D. was cutting into his serving of chicken-fried steak, his attention on his food.

Anger with him and with herself for her erotic musings added to her frustrations. She glared at the steam rising from the hot brew before her.

Annie nudged her with an elbow. "Lighten up, Doc. We're here to have fun."

"You're here to give me a hard time," Susan corrected.

"That's the fun part." Annie grinned and tossed her mop of fiery red curls.

"Where's that cherry cobbler?" she demanded, joining in the merriment. "I won't leave without it, and a big helping of ice cream melting on top."

The rich dessert arrived, and Carey again found J.D.'s eyes on her when she picked up the spoon. He watched while she took a bite of the luscious treat. The smile appeared at the corners of his mouth.

She thought of all the places he might kiss her as she licked ice cream off her lips….

Heat erupted all over her body at once. She couldn't decide if it was anger, embarrassment or just plain wild, lustful longing. Not that it particularly mattered. She had no time for any of them. Or for a cowboy with eyes that promised paradise.

"Look, Doc is having a hot flash," Annie, the irreverent, declared, pointing at the moisture that had collected on Carey's upper lip and forehead.

"It's the cobbler," one of the others piped up. "It's so delicious I'm getting erotic thoughts, too."

Annie eyed her fat-free sherbet in disgust, then grinned slyly. "Maybe I'd better order two servings of cobbler to take home. Bill needs all the help he can get—"

"I don't want to know about it," Susan stated firmly. "After all, I'm about to become a blushing bride."

"I hear the other guys in the lab are betting on when

you and Ken will surface after the ceremony. They give Ken three days at the most, then he'll have to get out of the house for some rest. They're thinking of renting a motel room so he can grab some sleep."

"He'll need it," Susan declared.

This drew another knowing "Aah" from the group before they dissolved into another round of laughter. They were still teasing the nurse about taking it easy on her husband-to-be when Carey left.

She saw that J.D. had already finished and was gone when she paid. He'd slipped out while her group was giving Susan a hard time over the nuptials, which would take place on Valentine's Day.

Valentine's Day—five weeks away. Christmas had passed in its usual whirl of pine boughs, tinsel and colored lights. A new year had begun, and she could barely recall the previous one—

"Oh." She laid a hand over her pounding heart as a tall, lanky form stepped out of the shadows.

"It's okay," J. D. Cade told her in his gravelly voice. "I didn't see your car and thought you might need a ride."

Carey was surprised that he'd noticed. Obviously he'd been silently watching her as much as she'd been watching him.

"No, thanks. I have to go back to the hospital. I left my car there."

He nodded and pulled his Stetson farther down on his forehead. "The wind is picking up. There might be snow before morning." He fell into step beside her.

"Maybe. Maybe not." For some reason, she stubbornly refused to agree with him.

She rammed her hands into the pockets of her old parka, bought at a closeout sale at the Army-Navy Store five years ago. The same went for the cardigan she wore and the gloves she'd forgotten somewhere. She was bad about losing things. She could never remember putting gloves and such down, and so couldn't remember where to find them.

"I really don't need an escort," she said.

"A woman shouldn't be alone on the streets after dark. It could be dangerous."

"In Whitehorn?" Her tone was openly scoffing.

The only danger she sensed came from him and the odd longing that made her want to crawl into his arms and stay there while passion flashed between them like heat lightning until they were both consumed. Lordy.

"Bad things have happened here," he reminded her.

The wind whipped the low statement away with a shriek as they turned the corner of the building at the end of the block. She staggered when the gale hit her full force in the face.

Her unsought companion looped an arm over her shoulders and tucked her in beside him, using his greater bulk to partly shield her from nature's fury. She felt instantly warmer. And safer. Which was odd, because she'd never felt less than at ease in the town. Nearly everyone knew her. After all, she'd grown up here.

"Bad things happen everywhere," she offered softly, sensing things from his past that he wouldn't share.

He gave a growl of agreement.

"What happened to your voice?" she asked.

As a doctor, she knew that several things could cause thickening of the vocal cords so that the tone was deeper and rougher than normal. One was long-term smoking. Another was straining an already swollen, inflamed throat as singers often did during concert tours. Scar tissue could form and ruin the voice forever.

She felt the tension coil in him, then release. He didn't pretend he didn't know what she meant.

"Screaming," he said.

"Vietnam," she guessed. "You were captured?"

"For a while." His tone was repressive.

"Sometimes it helps to talk—"

"I got over it."

She cast an assessing glance up at him. Maybe he had. A good sign was the fact that he seemed to have found a couple of friends in town. Sam Brightwater, for one. Reed Austin for another. An Indian and a cop, both firmly rooted in the community. It was a strange mix for a loner.

"How old were you when you shipped over?"

"If you're angling for my age, it's forty-three." His smile flashed in the dim glow of a streetlight. "Old enough for you."

"Huh. Maybe I think you're too old. I'm thirty-two."

"I know. Lily Mae Wheeler told me."

Carey groaned internally. "If Lily Mae cornered you at the café, I'm sure you know all about my life."

He laughed at her irritation. "I invited her to have coffee with me, then I proceeded to ask her about you."

Carey stopped at the entrance to the hospital parking lot. Visiting hours were over and only staff and those unlucky enough to be keeping long, lonely vigils beside their loved ones were still there.

"Why?" she demanded.

"Because."

He clasped her arm and guided her to the four-wheel-drive sports utility vehicle she had recently bought when her fifteen-year-old compact had gasped its last breath and refused to start again.

She realized she liked old, familiar things around her. Her compact had been a trusted friend. The ute was too new for her to know how it behaved in different weather and road conditions. She glanced at the man beside her.

How would he react in passion? Rough? Impatient? She didn't consider him a gentle man, but she instinctively knew he would handle a woman carefully.

He waited without one sign of impatience while she fished the keys out of the oversized bag she carried.

"Here." She handed him a packet of pills, then unlocked the door.

"What are these?"

"A sample pack of vitamins. Salesmen are always loading me up with pills. I ran into one when I stopped at the drugstore to pick up a card for a friend."

J.D. grunted and stuck the packet in his pocket. His hands settled on her shoulders before she could leap into the ute and be off. She saw the intent in his eyes before he bent his head toward her.

"Don't," she whispered. Panic eddied around her.

"Why?"

"Because."

He smiled at her use of his laconic term. "Afraid?"

"No." She knew that he knew she lied. "It would be pointless. An affair is out of the question."

"Is it?"

She huffed in irritation at the question. "Of course," she began strongly, then stopped, uncertain what she wanted to say next. The words were swept away on the wind.

He shifted so she was shielded from its force, then his breath caressed her lips as he leaned forward. She froze like a rabbit caught in the headlights of an oncoming car.

"How about a ride back to my truck?" he asked.

The words freed her to move. She turned her head. "At the café?"

"Yeah."

"Hop in. I have to get home." She remembered there was no one at the house waiting for her.

He walked around and climbed in the passenger side. She cranked the engine to let it warm, then fumbled with the seat belt.

He twisted sideways and caught her hands. "Let me do it. Your hands are like ice."

His, she noticed, were warm, yet he hadn't worn gloves, either. Warm hands, cold heart?

He didn't fasten the buckle. Instead, he unzipped his coat and guided her hands inside, up under his arms so she could soak up his body heat. She didn't draw away. She knew she should. She told herself to. But she didn't.

"You're like a furnace," she said. Her attempt at a laugh was breathless. Oh, help, she sounded like a teenager in the presence of a rock idol.

"So are you."

He slipped his hands inside her coat and lightly grasped her waist. His thumbs slid back and forth over her sweater. She swallowed a moan.

The parking-lot lighting created interesting shadows and points of brilliance in the dim interior of the ute. She saw his head move toward her. The light concentrated in his eyes for a second, then winked out. She realized he'd closed his eyes.

His lips touched hers.

The electric jolt went clear to her toes. Heat flowed between J.D. and Carey. She knew all the things she should do—pull back, berate him, get her own shaky emotions in hand. She knew—oh, yes, she knew. She didn't do any of them.

She let her hands glide over him, along his sides and up his torso. He lifted his arms, letting her explore where she would, then clamped down, trapping her hands against his body again. The heat was incredible. It melted any resistance she might have made.

His lips moved over hers, gently at first, then harder as the kiss became complicated, a thing of growing passion, of lips and tongue and teeth, of light touches and deep explorations and shimmering sensations.

The moan she'd suppressed escaped in a demanding tone of need. He drew her closer, deeper into his embrace.

She slipped her arms around him. Their knees hit. He

wedged an arm under her legs and lifted them over his lap so that her thighs rested on his. Then he trailed his hand up her leg on the return journey. He didn't stop at her waist, but slid under her sweater with a sure touch.

Her breath caught when his hand cupped her breast and kneaded it in his supple fingers. A sound like the keening of the wind rushed through her. She heard their quick breaths and knew the wonder of shared desire.

Somewhere inside her, knowledge grew. The months she'd spent avoiding him since he'd shown up in town had come down to this moment in his arms. Each chance meeting of their eyes, each accidental touch, had proclaimed the inevitable—that sooner or later, she'd end up here, like this.

"You taste of wine and cherry cobbler," he murmured on a half laugh.

He licked at her lips, driving her mindless with the unappeased hunger he incited in her, and it was on the tip of her tongue to invite him to her house. With Sophie away, there was no one to witness her indiscretion, no one to face but her own accusing eyes in the morning. She clamped her teeth into her bottom lip to hold the words in while he kissed along her neck.

He pushed the bulky cardigan aside and kissed down to the vee of the sweater she wore underneath it. He eased the knitted material over until he could kiss the swell of her breast. With careful expertise, he pulled her bra down and tasted the passion-hardened nipple.

She moved against him. Her thigh came in contact with the hard shaft contained by his jeans. He groaned her name, his deep, raspy voice exciting her as much as his touch. She pressed closer, harder, to that warm strength.

It would be so easy to let it happen. Mindless bliss. A few hours of forgetfulness. And then?

She frowned, not wanting to think beyond the moment. Slipping her hands around his neck, she held him to her breast while he laved and sucked at the engorged tip. She caressed him until he clasped her knee and held her still against him.

"Enough," he warned, "or I'll take you right here."

She nearly invited him to do so. Or maybe her actions had done that for her. They watched each other warily, their faces only inches apart, their breaths mingling as they sought control.

The wind hit the truck with renewed force, rocking it on the extra-wide, thick-treaded tires she'd bought for winter driving. She needed something firm and dependable under her for stability at this moment. He shifted and his rock-hard thighs flexed under her as if offering that solid base she so desperately needed.

"We'd better go. I need to get home." She cleared the huskiness from her throat.

He didn't argue. Instead, he carefully adjusted her bra, then the sweater, to cover her breast. Each touch of his fingers was like a lick of fire against her skin. She'd never been so sensitive, so aware of a man, in her life.

When she moved her legs, he let her go and slid over to his side of the vehicle, pulling his Stetson back into place. He continued to study her for a long, silent minute.

With trembling fingers, she fastened the seat belt,

then put the truck into reverse. She realized she couldn't see out the rear window. All the windows were covered with a dense fog.

"Worse than a couple of teenagers," she muttered, her anger directed more at herself than him. "Steaming up the place." She turned the fan and heat on high. The fog didn't clear.

He reached over and flicked the air-conditioning on with the heat. "That should clear it faster."

It did. She adjusted the temperature as the windows cleared, then she backed out. "You need to fasten your seat belt."

"It's too late," he said. "I've already crashed."

She flicked a grimace his way. He grinned, reached across his chest with his left hand and snapped the buckle in place with the skill of one who was ambidextrous.

"Very funny." She headed away from the hospital before remembering she'd intended to look at the test results once more. Gloom settled around her shoulders. What for? The prognosis was as clear as a laser printer could make it.

"What's wrong?" J.D. asked.

"What?"

"You sighed."

"Oh. It's nothing."

"Just the weight of the world on your shoulders, huh?" he said, mocking her short answer. "Fortunately for us lesser mortals, you medical types can carry it."

She shot him a warning glance. "I'm in no mood for your rancor."

"Your moods change fast. Two minutes ago, you were in the mood for some pretty heavy—"

"That was a mistake, one that won't happen again."

"A mistake," he repeated. "Well, glad to get that cleared up. I sure as hell thought it was passion."

She gave an audible huff. Her head was beginning to pound again. Thank God they were at the restaurant. She whipped into an empty parking space on the street and hoped no cop saw her parked facing in the wrong direction—the police station and courthouse were down the street.

"Don't go highfalutin on me," he ordered. "You were giving as good as you were getting."

An unexpected chuckle brought her head around. She glared and waited for him to climb out.

"And it was damn good," he declared. With that, he opened the door and swung to the ground.

She tore out before he'd hardly stepped back and slammed the door. She hit the button that locked her inside the warm truck and drove straight home. The light was on at the house. Lorrie—Lorenza Garcia, her housekeeper and baby-sitter—had left it on for her.

After parking in the garage, Carey went into the homey warmth of birch paneling and knitted afghans on overstuffed sofas, a wood-burning fireplace and... emptiness.

She glanced in Sophie's room as she passed, even though she knew the child was spending the night with a friend. Carey smiled wryly as she changed into a warm flannel nightgown. Maybe the five-year-old would make it fine through the night, but would her thirty-two-year-old mom manage to get any sleep?

Seeing that it was only ten after nine, she made a fire in the grate and prepared a cup of hot chocolate. Seated in front of the crackling blaze, she thought over the evening and wondered why she'd let herself fall into J. D. Cade's arms like that.

She just wasn't that type of woman. Passion—or to put it bluntly, sex—had never been that important to her. Her daughter and her profession came first in her life. Really, that was all she had time for.

Tomorrow was going to be a rough day. She was going to drop by the McCallum home at eleven. Oh, God, she dreaded it. She set the mug of cocoa aside and covered her face. For a moment, she wished she had a pair of strong arms around her. She wished for kisses and caresses that would drive out all thoughts of tomorrow. It would be harder not to think of those things in the future now that she knew there was one man whose touch could do that very thing.

Why, oh, why, had she let herself respond to a drifter like J. D. Cade even for a moment?

Madness, that's what it had been. And maybe loneliness, too. A little. But it wasn't something she wanted to admit.

She sighed and listened to the wind outside the house. Inside, there was only the merry snap of the fire to keep her company.

Two

"Umm, love you." Carey nuzzled her daughter's neck above the fleecy sweater.

Sophie gave her a milk-damp kiss on the cheek. "Love you, too." She'd joined Carey for a second breakfast when she'd arrived home from the sleepover.

Carey straightened and spoke to Lorrie. "I'll be home around noon, I think. I only have one appointment this morning after my rounds."

"Sophie is invited to the Saturday matinee at the Roxy. Dina's mom is picking her up," Lorrie reminded her.

"Oh, that's right. I'll have lunch in town. Why don't you take off when Carol comes by for Sophie? I'll be here when she gets back."

"Unless there's an emergency." Lorrie smiled in understanding of a doctor's life.

Carey thought of Jennifer McCallum. "Unless there's an emergency," she echoed. She pulled her favorite cardigan on, slung her purse over her shoulder and left the warm kitchen. She honked after she backed out of the garage. Sophie waved her spoon at the window.

As soon as she was on the road, Carey felt the weight of worry drop on her again. Childhood leukemia had over a ninety-percent survival rate. Usually. However, they had already tried Jennifer on chemotherapy. The test results had shown it hadn't worked, not as they needed it to.

She parked in her usual spot and rushed to the double doors of the hospital. She didn't want to remember how wanton she'd acted the previous night, making out in the hospital parking lot. Stupid, really stupid.

In the staff room, she stored her purse and cardigan in her locker and slipped a green surgery gown on over her T-shirt before stopping by the nurses' station.

"Hi," Annie greeted her. Her mop of red hair was contained in two thick braids this morning. "Everything is under control. Rachel Parma lost her breakfast, so we switched back to a liquid diet. She kept down six ounces of soda and four of Jell-O."

"Good." Carey picked up the charts for her patients and went through each one before beginning her rounds.

Annie joined her when she was relieved at the desk. Together they examined and joked with the twelve children in the pediatric wing.

During the holidays, the medical staff had tried to

send everyone home, if at all possible. So far, there'd been only a couple of tonsillectomies admitted in this, the first month of the new year.

"Hi, Dr. Hall, can I go home today?" her third patient demanded, as he had each morning that week.

"Yep."

The ten-year-old looked so surprised it made her laugh.

"Really? I can?"

"Yes. You've driven Annie to the point where she told me just this morning, either that kid in 4B goes or I go. It was an easy choice. You're outa here. Call your mom and tell her to pick you up in an hour."

She got a high five, then a choke-hold hug, before she moved on. She dismissed the two tonsil kids with a stern admonition to take it easy for a week and eat lots of ice cream. That always made them laugh.

It was the last patient in the ward who had her worried. An eighteen-year-old who seemingly had the world at her feet couldn't keep any solid food down. Involuntary bulimia. The girl had lost thirty pounds since the beginning of the school year. Technically, the patient shouldn't have been in pediatrics, but Carey had been her doctor for six years.

"Hey, Rachel," Carey greeted the patient. "Annie says you kept some soda and Jell-O down this morning."

Rachel gave her a wan smile. "Finally."

"That's good news." Carey sat on the side of the bed and took the girl's hand. "Tell me about your summer. Did you break up with your boyfriend?" she asked softly.

Rachel's chin quivered as she shook her head.

Carey thought she must have hit a sore spot. She sent Annie a look that asked her to leave. Annie glanced at her watch, mumbled something indistinct and rushed out.

"So what's eating at you?" Carey asked when she was alone with the patient she'd known since birth. "We've run a bunch of tests, all negative. Do you have any idea what we should be looking for?"

Rachel pleated the sheet between nervous fingers for a long, tense moment before she answered. "Did you do a pregnancy test?" The words were hardly audible.

Carey almost dropped the chart. Rachel was a straight-A student, had been secretary of her high-school class and was now on the student council at college. Carey had expected boyfriend problems or worries about her grades—college was a hard transition for some kids—but not this.

"Why don't we do the test and see how it goes before we worry ourselves to death about it?" she suggested.

Rachel caught her arm. "Don't tell anyone, please."

Carey patted the hand that clutched her so desperately. "I'm your doctor. Whatever we say is confidential. Even from parents," she added, and saw the swift look of relief on the youngster's face. "I'll stick with you through whatever happens."

That broke the dam of worry that had prevented Rachel from keeping any food down. She told Carey everything.

Rachel was at college on a scholarship. To lose it would bring shame and disgrace on her parents. All their hopes for the future were pinned on their bright but vulnerable child.

Carey sighed as she walked down the corridor an hour later. She'd been lucky to have parents who didn't live their lives through their children, who had expected goodness and decency and a reasonable level of accomplishment, but not the impossible from their kids.

Rachel's parents hadn't prepared their smart, earnest daughter for the senior who was president of the student body. He'd found the freshman an easy mark for his charm. He'd used her, then dropped her when his old girlfriend had decided to take him back.

Rachel, alone and desolate, had worried herself into being ill. She wasn't pregnant, only ashamed of being foolish and falling for the first line she heard.

"We have three going home today and one tomorrow," Annie remarked when Carey joined her at the desk.

"You read my mind. I was just thinking how much better it is for children to be home, if possible."

"They need their families." Annie put the charts away and leaned against the end of the desk, where the other RN talked on the phone. "Is Sophie at her dad's place for the weekend?"

"No, we're staying around here. By the way, I've signed the final papers on the ranch, and it's really ours. Sophie thinks it's a great adventure to stay at the old Baxter cabin and hike around in the hills, so we're taking off three days next weekend to explore the place."

"How does it feel to own your own spread? Do you have any cattle yet?"

Carey laughed. "Not one scrawny cow on the place. I've wondered why the Kincaid trustees never put cattle over there. I guess they never got around to it." She shrugged.

"Yeah. Have you any news on Jennifer McCallum?"

Carey didn't answer for a couple of seconds. "I have an appointment with Sterling and Jessica this morning."

Annie pressed her lips together. "Not good, huh?"

"No, it isn't good." Carey shoved the charts into their racks. "I'm off now. I won't be back in tonight or tomorrow unless you need me."

"Okay. Have a nice weekend."

"You, too."

Carey stripped out of the green shirt and left it in the laundry bin, then retrieved her purse and sweater before heading for the door.

Brr, it was really cold outside, but no sign of snow yet. She unlocked the truck and hopped in. After glancing at her watch, she decided against stopping for coffee. She'd go on over to the McCallum place now.

The house was set back from the road on a quiet street. The broad front porch lent it a friendly appearance. The couple had added onto the place after adopting Jenny.

Carey parked behind the unmarked patrol car that Sterling used. She sat there for a second before climbing down. They were waiting for her. The door opened as soon as she walked up on the porch.

"Hello. Come in," Jessica invited. "Let me take your...oh, you don't have a coat. It's freezing out today." She looked rather at a loss.

"Hi, Jessica." Carey pulled the cardigan off and let Jessica hang it in the coat closet. "I keep a parka in the truck in case I need it. Lost my gloves, though."

"Sit by the fire and warm up. I have spiced cider. Would you like some?"

"Yes, please. Ah, this feels good. Sterling, how are you?" She shook hands with the special investigator.

"Fine. You'd better find your gloves. It's supposed to stay around freezing the entire weekend."

"I'll pick up some at the Army-Navy Store."

Carey accepted the mug of hot cider from Jessica and took a sip before setting it aside. Jessica and Sterling looked at her. She saw fear in Jessica's eyes. Sterling, good cop that he was, showed nothing, but there had been a frown on his face since they'd brought Jenny in for a checkup because the child had grown listless and had little appetite. That's when the illness had been discovered.

"The news isn't good," she began.

Sterling slipped his right arm around Jessica's shoulders and took her left hand in his. A loving, united force, Carey observed, and was amazed at the envy she experienced. Jack hadn't been there for her, not even when their daughter was born and Carey had hemorrhaged. She shoved the memory aside.

"The chemotherapy didn't quite work as we had hoped. However, there're other treatments," she quickly added as the blood drained out of Jessica's face and Sterling's frown became fierce.

"What do we need to do?" he asked.

"I talked to Kane Hunter and we've decided upon another therapy. It's hard on a child. And parents."

Kane, a senior staff physician and member of the medical board at the hospital, was also a friend of the McCallums. Carey thought it would make them feel better to know he was the hospital adviser on the case.

"What is it?" Sterling asked impatiently.

"We would have to destroy her bone marrow. A three-year-old is particularly vulnerable to the side effects of chemotherapy, so she's close to that point now. We consulted with one of the country's foremost oncologists at the cancer center in Seattle. He agrees that a bone marrow transplant should be done right away if we can get a good match. We'll need a relative, if possible."

Jessica drew a shaky breath. "Clint Calloway is a half brother. That's the only relative Jenny has."

"Thanks to Lexine Baxter," Sterling muttered.

His tone sent a chill down Carey's spine. Cold fury gleamed in his dark eyes. Lexine was lucky to be safely in prison. Carey knew the full story of Lexine Baxter and her plans to get total control of the Kincaid holdings by posing as Mary Jo Plummer, a sweet, unassuming children's librarian, and by marrying Dugin Kincaid. The woman had fooled the whole town...until it came out she'd murdered Jeremiah Kincaid, her father-in-law and Baby Jennifer's natural father, as well as her husband, poor, spineless Dugin Kincaid. Clint, like Jenny, was another of Jeremiah's illegitimate offspring.

"There're probably a dozen Kincaid bastards in this state alone," Sterling said. "If we could only find them."

"My thoughts exactly." Carey met the lawman's hard gaze and knew they were in agreement about their opinion of the Kincaid family, including Lexine, who'd married into it. "Is Jenny asleep?"

Jessica spoke up. "Yes. Do you want to see her?"

Carey shook her head. She did, but only to reassure herself. "Bring her in Monday." She dug her day planner out of her heavy purse. "We'll need to get some blood samples and start the final tests. Can you come in then?"

"So soon?" Jessica looked stricken.

"I want to start as soon as possible. Delay won't do Jenny any good."

"I know. It just makes it so real and terrible. She's only three. Hardly more than a baby."

Sterling's arm tightened around his wife. He kissed her temple and made a soothing sound. Carey swallowed the lump in her throat at the gentle signs of his love. Her eyes stung. She wrote the appointment in her book and stood. "I have to go. I'll see you Monday at noon."

"Won't you have lunch with us?" Jessica invited.

"No, thanks." She squeezed Jessica's arm reassuringly, retrieved her cardigan and left the warm atmosphere of the McCallum house.

She drove down Center Street and decided to have lunch at the café before going home. She resisted the urge to drop in at the Roxy and attend the movie with Sophie. Being a good parent also meant knowing when to let go. Sophie was developing her own circle of friends.

It was early, so she had no problem finding a seat at

the Hip Hop. Filled with thoughts of Jenny and the upcoming treatment, she didn't notice the other occupants until she heard laughter that strummed over her nerves like velvet on glass, setting up an electric current.

J.D. sat at the counter, the same place he'd chosen last night. He and the waitress were chatting and laughing. The waitress was openly flirting with him, giving him come-on glances from beneath lashes that were as fake as those worn by Lily Mae Wheeler, the town gossip, who sat at a nearby table with two other women. Three other tables were also occupied by talkative groups, all having fun.

Carey frowned at the menu detailing the day's specials. She resented the other diners' merriment. Life was serious. It was hard and unfair and uncaring— To her dismay, tears stung her eyes again. She sniffed discreetly and tried to think of things other than the dire future of her three-year-old patient.

When the young waitress finally came to the table, Carey ordered the vegetable platter and a glass of milk. Then she gazed out the window and watched the freezing wind blow the treetops in the town park.

A figure loomed beside her.

"Mind if I join you?"

J.D. took a seat and plunked a coffee mug on the table.

"It looks as if you already have," she said irritably.

"Who pulled your tail this morning?"

Amusement flashed in the sky-blue eyes as he asked the question and make no move to leave, although it should have been obvious she didn't want company.

A stray beam of sunlight snuck out from behind the gathering clouds, lighting the world to momentary brilliance and centering in his eyes before disappearing.

Jennifer McCallum was the only other person she'd ever seen who had eyes as impossibly blue as J.D.'s. And Jenny's natural father, Jeremiah Kincaid. Dugin Kincaid had also had blue eyes, but his had always seemed a washed-out shade of blue. A cynical thought came to her—maybe J.D. was another illegitimate son.

She sighed and thought of Clint Calloway. She'd call him that afternoon and see if he'd be willing to come in for blood tests to see if he matched with Jennifer. Six blood factors had to be checked.

"There's that heavy sigh again," J.D. remarked. "I like to hear that from a woman after we've had fantastic sex. Other times, it's just plain worrisome. Trouble with a patient?" he asked.

She flicked her attention to him, amazed at his insight. He even had the grace to look concerned.

An act?

He always seemed such a lone wolf she didn't expect him to have much feeling for other people and their distress, or to bother getting involved.

"Yes."

"I'll listen." He sipped his coffee.

"Don't you have work to do? Does your foreman know you're hanging out here all the time?"

He grinned in that lazy way he had that made her think of other things…like kissing and laughing and making love. Oh, God, she really was going around the bend.

"I'm in town on ranch business. The flatbed we use to haul hay is being repaired. If this winter ends as bad as it started, we'll need every bale to feed the cattle. I'm waiting for the mechanic to call me when the work is finished. Does that meet with your approval, Miss Kitty, ma'am?"

She looked down at her plain duds and compared them to the fancy clothes of the saloon owner in the old *Gunsmoke* series on TV. Miss Kitty had also worn false eyelashes.

"You got the wrong woman, cowboy," she drawled. "The saloon is over on the main highway."

He chuckled, then his eyes narrowed as he studied her. "You'd dress up real nice, though. Your eyes are pretty, and your skin is softer than a cat's belly."

The waitress brought the milk and set it down none too gently. "Easy, there, Janie," J.D. cautioned, flicking the girl a glance that held annoyance as well as amusement.

A flush highlighted the girl's cheeks as she flounced off. Carey recalled an article in the paper a couple of weeks ago. Janie's brother, Dale Carson, was wanted for questioning in connection with some skulduggery at the Kincaid ranch.

"Anyone heard from her brother?" Carey asked now, her sympathy going to the girl.

"No, he's disappeared. I'd sure like to know who he was working for."

Carey raised her eyebrows. "What makes you think he was working for someone?"

"Dale's bright, but nowhere smart enough to have pulled this off alone. There's been systematic destruction going on at the ranch for the past two years. When the trustees sold you part of the old Baxter holdings, it was because of a cash-flow problem. The operation has had a steady cash draw down for nearly three years. With the price of beef where it is, the ranch won't make it through another disastrous year."

"It would be so odd," she murmured.

"What?"

"Not to have the Kincaid ranch. It's been here over a hundred years—one of those things you take for granted, like those three peaks in the Crazy Mountains."

He stared into the steam rising from his cup. "The Baxters were one of the first families in the area, too. They're also gone. Maybe it's for the best. Let the old blood die out and the new take over."

"The end of a dynasty. It seems so sad."

"From what I hear, neither Jeremiah nor Dugin were very much missed by anyone."

She sipped her milk thoughtfully, puzzled by the bitterness in J.D.'s tone. "Wayne was the golden boy," she said on a soft note. "I had a crush on him when I was about eight."

"Good God," he muttered in disgust.

"He ran into me as I was coming out of the store. I dropped my ice-cream cone. He bought me another. That was, umm, a week before he ran off and joined the service. He never came back from 'Nam. It nearly killed Jeremiah."

"Huh," J.D. scoffed.

"I think Wayne was the one person he truly loved."

The silence stretched between them as she thought of love and all its manifestations, good and bad.

"There're different kinds of love. Kincaid sounds like a selfish bastard to me. He only wanted his son to reflect glory on him," J.D. told her, his tone dropping so low she had to strain to hear. "A boy will do anything to please his father. Until he finds out what a fool he is for thinking the old man is perfect when everyone else knows what the kid doesn't—that his dad is a first-class bastard."

"Was your father like that?"

"He lied and cheated on my mother and laughed when she found out. Her tears didn't mean a thing to him—"

Carey looked at J.D. in sympathy when he stopped abruptly. He appeared angry, as if he'd given too much of himself away.

"It hurts to find your idol has clay feet," she said understandingly. "Perhaps you were too hard on him."

"You don't know a damn thing about it," he said so fiercely she drew back, startled.

"You're right." She glanced at her watch. "I wonder what's holding up the kitchen. I want to go home and take a nap while I have the house to myself."

His anger cooled, then faded. "I could use a nap myself," he suggested, his insolent grin kicking up the corners of his mouth.

His gaze settled on her T-shirt, and she felt her breasts growing hard, the way they had last night when he'd nibbled and sucked at them.

"You could invite me over," he added.

"I doubt if I'd get any sleep."

His grin widened, and she realized she'd stepped right into that one. She brushed a strand of hair off her face impatiently. "I prefer to sleep alone."

"You didn't at one time—else you wouldn't have a kid."

"I don't discuss my marriage."

"And that's that," he said, mocking her statement.

She gave him a level stare.

His tone became intimate. "Did you make the same sounds for your husband that you made for me last night?"

"Passion is much the same with one man as another," she announced. As if she were an expert in the field. Like Rachel, she'd been an easy mark for a charming man.

Jack had evidently seen her as a meal ticket for life when she'd filed for a divorce. Luckily, with a marriage that had lasted slightly less than three years, the judge hadn't thought that entitled her ex-husband to alimony and half of her assets, especially when he was the one to leave.

She sighed, thinking of Sterling McCallum and his concern for Jessica and their daughter. Lucky woman. For some couples, such as her parents, their love grew and deepened over the years. It must be nice—

"Heavy sigh, third one." J.D. quirked one dark brown eyebrow at her. "What's wrong?"

"PMS," she stated, deadpan.

He blinked, then erupted into laughter. "No, it isn't. If it were, you would die before you admitted it to me."

She grudgingly smiled. He was right about that.

"We strike sparks—" He was interrupted by the arrival of her food.

"More coffee?" Janie asked. She set the plate in front of Carey and glared at J.D. as if she would just as soon pour it over his head.

"Yeah. Thanks." He edged back from the table.

When the girl left, Carey lofted an eyebrow in his direction. "Am I encroaching on another woman's territory?"

"Hardly. I'm a little old for teenagers." He shot an irritated glance after the girl. "And I haven't led her on, either, so don't hit me with that one."

"Poor man, so put upon." She picked up her fork, delighted at seeing him discomposed for once.

"Damn right. You women know how to make life rough for a man. The kid falls all over me, but the woman I want…" He paused for emphasis. "Who also wants me, holds back for reasons she won't discuss."

Aghast, she looked around to make sure no one had overheard his accusation. "You have an incredible ego."

"Yeah? Tell me this. What happened between us last night? Was that a figment of my imagination?"

"No, it was a mistake. One that I don't intend to let happen again."

"How are you going to stop it," he demanded, his voice dropping to a verbal caress, his eyes gleaming wickedly, "when you want it as much as I do?"

"I don't—" She couldn't bring herself to lie. Instead, she laughed lightly. "You're everything I don't want in a man—you're a drifter, basically a loner, as dependable as a night fog. And like the fog, when morning comes you'll be gone. Why would I involve myself with a man like that?"

She saw that she'd gotten to him. A dull flush crept up his neck. His lips, sensuous and mobile, thinned to a taut line.

"Because you'll have missed something special, the way it was last night when it was just you and me and nothing else." He settled back in the chair and looked her over slowly and deliberately. "You know the trouble with you?"

"I'm sure you're going to tell me," she said wryly, and waited for him to do so.

"You think too much. You should try going with your instincts sometimes. I find mine seldom tell me wrong."

"Like when it's time to move on?" She gave him a big-eyed, mockingly innocent stare before she finished the last of her vegetables.

"Yeah. Like then."

"Carey." Susan came in the door, saw her and rushed over. "I heard about Jennifer, that the chemotherapy didn't work. Is it true?"

Carey was knocked back into the real world with a thud. She'd momentarily forgotten her worries in the male-female verbal sparring with him. "I'm afraid so."

"Are you talking about the McCallum kid?" J.D. broke in, a curious expression in his eyes.

Carey nodded. "She'll be stopping by the hospital on Monday around noon," she said to the pediatric nurse. "We'll finish the chemotherapy, then…"

"Then?" J.D. snapped.

"Then we see if Clint Calloway is a possible blood marrow donor."

"What happens if he isn't?"

Carey gazed into eyes as blue as the Arctic sea. He seemed intent upon her answer. "We'll have to go outside the family to see if we can get a matchup."

Susan clucked sympathetically. "I'll be watching for Jenny on Monday. I'll tell Annie to stay close. Jenny knows her. That'll make the child feel better if she sees someone she knows."

"I suspect Jessica will go into isolation with Jenny when the time comes."

The nurse said goodbye and joined her party.

Carey pushed her plate aside and sipped her milk. She drew a deep breath and let it out slowly.

"Now I know what the sighs are about," J.D. murmured.

His expression, she noticed, was different from any he'd ever bestowed on her, although she couldn't say how it differed.

"And no doubt you're going to tell me," she quipped dryly. She thought of life, of death, of how short one could be and how prolonged the other.

"You're worried about Jennifer McCallum."

"She's only three." The awful sting of tears surprised her again. What was wrong with her nowadays?

He nodded. "I'd take her place if I could. Do you believe me?"

Oddly, she did. She didn't know why. "Yes."

He reached for her hand and squeezed it in his. She looked at his long, aristocratic fingers. Her own hands, with their short, blunt nails, appeared plebeian next to his. She touched the calluses on his palm. "You have surgeon's hands."

"I'd once thought of going into medicine."

"Why didn't you?"

He released her. "I went to war, instead."

If he felt regret over that decision, it didn't show in his voice or face. It was just a statement of fact, nothing more, nothing less.

She nodded, knowing he'd left his home for reasons he'd buried long ago. Pity stirred. She shook her head, aware how foolish that was.

"I don't want or need your pity," he said softly, reading her mind.

"Consider it a gift." She laid a ten on the table, pulled on her cardigan and left.

Three

Wayne Kincaid, alias J. D. Cade, pulled on the string of barbed wire, cleated it to the post, then checked the tautness by giving it a twang. It felt about right.

He strung the other four wires of the stock fence, then took off his hat and blotted the sweat from his forehead with a swipe of his sleeve. The temperature wasn't quite forty degrees Fahrenheit, but the air was still and the sun was out.

The warm rays had felt good earlier, but now he was hot. He dropped his tools in the back of the truck and sat on the tailgate. He pulled out his lunch but didn't open the bag. Instead, he grabbed a beer from the cooler and settled back against the truck, then gazed at the mountains. This was about the prettiest spot in all creation.

A ridge of cap rock formed the boundary between

the old Baxter place and the Kincaid spread. It brought back memories—riding and hiking parties with friends, hunting with his dad…back when he'd still thought his father was the perfect man, when he'd thought he had to live up to that perfect image and be the hero his dad demanded of his sons.

If he hadn't caught his father in the act with another woman, he wondered how long he would have continued thinking the old man was right up there next to God in wisdom.

That day in the stable had opened his eyes.

"How could you, Dad? How could you do that?" he'd demanded, righteous as only a fifteen-year-old can be. "Mom saw you. She was crying."

His father had gotten furious at being questioned, then he'd laughed at his son's anguish. "Grow up," he'd ordered in a bellow. "Jesus, I run this whole f-ing outfit. A man needs to relax once in a while, to have some fun without his own family coming down on him. It doesn't mean anything."

The cowboy's wife who had been in the hay with his dad had clutched her chest as if she'd been stabbed with a knife. It had meant something to her.

And to him. That day had marked the end of unquestioning love and respect. It had marked the end of living up to the demands his old man made on him. It had marked the beginning of his observing life and thinking about things in his own way.

Then, at eighteen, just out of high school and planning on going to college to study medicine, which his father had sneered at, there had been a final quarrel when his father had been out of town at a time his mom took sick.

A strange woman had answered the phone when he'd called the hotel where the Cattlemen's Association convention was taking place. His father's voice had been slurred when he came on the line.

Drunk and whoring again. Wayne had hung up in disgust and stayed with his mother at the hospital. He'd signed papers and authorized treatment as if he were the responsible adult.

He'd also made a vow—he was going to kill his father when he showed up.

His mother had come through the minor heart attack and, seeing what was in his eyes, had begged him not to quarrel with his father. "Then I'll have to leave," he'd replied.

"Where would you go?"

"Anywhere. I don't care." He looked out the hospital window and saw two guys in uniforms. "The army. Will you sign for me?"

"Your father—"

"To hell with him! I'll take to the road. I'm heading for any state that doesn't have him in it."

She'd been silent, her eyes filled with anguish. "I'll sign for you to join the army if you promise to write every week. Every week, Wayne."

"I will. You should leave, too, Mom. You have friends back in Virginia. You could go back home."

She shook her head. "No, not yet. Later, maybe."

But she'd known her heart was weak. She'd lasted

another few years, then died as quietly as she'd lived, a gentle, refined woman who had loved the mountains. And Jeremiah Kincaid, although the bastard hadn't deserved it.

A noise in the underbrush drew him out of the bitter past and into the present. Freeway came limping across the dirt track that formed the road. He sat down and held up his paw with an expectant look.

"So you need some medical attention, huh? What did you pick up this time—another thorn?"

Wayne examined the huge paw of the mongrel that had adopted him years ago. Freeway's brows quirked in that worried manner dogs adopt when they're unsure about letting their human work on them.

"Whoa, that's a granddaddy of a thorn, buddy."

Freeway thumped his tail once.

"Hell, it's all the way through the pad. Okay, hold still. I'll try to pull it out."

He grasped the end of the thorn and tried to ease it out the way it went in. The end snapped off.

"Damn." There was nothing he could get ahold of now. The sharp end of the thorn barely protruded through the skin. He got out his knife.

Freeway took one look and hobbled off. The dog remembered the last time Wayne had used a knife to cut a porcupine quill out of his lip.

"Come back here, you chicken. It won't hurt much."

The dog sat down a good ten feet away—too far for Wayne to make a grab for him—and licked at his injured paw. He gave a surprised yelp when he hit the thorn.

"Don't say I didn't tell you. That has to come out." Wayne patted the tailgate. "Come on, I'll take you in to the vet. He'll fix you right up. Come on," he coaxed.

After a lot of damn fool cajoling on his part, Freeway finally limped over and let Wayne lift his ornery carcass into the truck.

Wayne was just about to close the back end, when he heard singing in the distance. Two people, a female and a child, he guessed, were coming down the mountain trail. He waited for them to come into sight.

"Will miracles never end?" he muttered when he saw Carey and her daughter stride around the boulder at the bend in the trail. "Hello," he called.

They both stopped. The child grinned and came bouncing on down the slope. The mother hesitated, then followed. If Carey could have grabbed her daughter and beat it back up the trail without looking ridiculous, he was pretty sure she would have. He grinned and let the pleasure roll over him.

That was a worrisome thing, too. He liked it more and more every time he saw her.

He wanted to touch her hair, which always had a tousled appearance, the short curls wafting enticingly around her temples, calling for a man's hands to smooth them into order…or more disorder. He wanted to touch her all over.

A coil of heat began unwinding inside him.

Her cheeks were pink from the hike, and her lips had a subtle shine. Maybe lip gloss. He couldn't recall ever seeing lipstick on her full, generous lips.

For a second, he recalled how they'd felt under his mouth last week, supple and soft and warm, moving with his movements, hungry the way he was hungry…

He stopped that line of thought as he felt a strain against his jeans. This wasn't the time.

Watch it, he ordered. A man could get in too deep before he knew it. However, he'd never met a woman he couldn't walk away from. For a painful moment, he recalled Kate Randall and his youthful love for her. He'd made promises back then, but fate—and his father—had forced him to break them up. He shook his head slightly, pushing the memory aside. Since leaving home, he'd wanted no ties. He'd always made that clear. He tried to play fair.

But she sure was a pretty woman. Proud and independent as hell, too. And scared of letting her feelings loose.

He could identify with that. He didn't want any emotional entanglements, either. Briefly he wondered if that made him just like his father.

The kid stopped in front of him. She was also cute. Cheeks pink as the first blush on an apple, a pug nose with a few freckles, brown eyes, long hair the same brown-blond shade as Carey's. The pair were obviously mother and daughter.

"What are you doing here?" Carey asked suspiciously.

"Mending fences." He pointed to the new strands of wire on the posts. "I was just going to pack it in, though. Freeway here has picked up a nasty thorn."

"My mom can fix it," the kid spoke up. "She can fix anything. Is your dog's name really Freeway?"

"Yup."

"Why?"

"That's where we teamed up, oh, six or seven years ago. We were heading in the same direction on the interstate…out in California, I think it was. We just sort of hung out together after that."

"I'm going to get a dog when I grow up. I'm going to name him Buzz. If I had two dogs, I could name the other one Woody." She gave her mother a significant glance.

"Disney characters," Carey explained to him. "You already have Pickles and Dudley. We're not home enough to take care of dogs," she told her daughter, her chin set in the same stubborn mode as the kid's. Like mother, like daughter, for sure.

He hid a grin.

"Lorrie is home all the time. Besides, I'd take care of them after school, Mom. I promise."

"Two cats are enough," Carey said.

"I had a dog when I grew up—" He stopped before he gestured toward the vast, lush valley that constituted the Kincaid land.

Close call, he warned himself. It was probably only a matter of time before everyone knew who he was, what with Sam Brightwater already figuring it out. And Kate, too. Others would probably catch on soon.

He looked at Carey, with her direct gaze and down-to-earth nature. She wasn't a woman to put up with subterfuge in a man, no matter how good the reason. For a second he tried to think of his excellent reasons for not telling anyone who he was, the foremost being that he didn't want the baggage that went with the Kincaid name. He'd been free of it for twenty-five years. There was no going back now.

"Come on, Sophie, we should let Mr. Cade get back to his work." Carey shifted restlessly like a runner toeing the mark, ready to be off at the sound of the gun.

Her attitude roused his own bullheadedness. He didn't like being silently declared unfit company. "I'm just having lunch. Care to join me?" He smiled in a real friendly fashion.

Carey's eyes narrowed.

"We have some, too," the kid piped up. "Let's eat here, Mom, okay? This is nice. I can play with Freeway."

The daughter gave her mom a look that would have melted Scrooge's heart without the ghostly visits.

"I don't think—"

"Good idea," he agreed. "Thinking is too much trouble on a day as beautiful as this." He moved aside. "Sit right here, ladies. I have soda in the cooler. Want one?"

"Please," Sophie said. She held up her arms.

He realized the kid expected him to pick her up and set her on the tailgate. He did. She was as light as a piece of thistledown. Her eyes conveyed the most complete trust in her world, and therefore in him, of anyone he'd ever seen. It brought an odd tightness to his chest.

"Hi, Freeway." Sophie patted his head and scratched around his ears.

"Careful," Wayne cautioned. "He might not be feeling friendly with that thorn in his paw." He fished a couple of cans of soda out of the cooler and handed them to the girls.

"Mom, can you fix Freeway now?" the kid asked with another of her soulful, pleading looks.

"I'll check it out. If that's okay with you?" Carey cast a questioning glance his way.

"Sure, but I don't have a needle or anything."

She smiled in the maddeningly practical manner of the trained professional. "I do." She swung a backpack off and pulled a well-equipped first-aid kit out.

"You could do surgery on the trail," he commented.

"If I had to," she said coolly. "Would you tie your handkerchief around his muzzle, please?"

"He won't bite."

"Maybe not voluntarily, but I'm a stranger and I'm going to hurt him. He might react instinctively. I'd rather be safe than sorry."

He saw her point. "Easy, boy," he murmured, yanking his handkerchief from around his neck. He looped it around Freeway's muzzle and behind his ears so it wouldn't come off easily. The dog appeared rather surprised at this strange treatment, but he didn't fight it.

Carey looked at the injured paw, pressed on it a couple of times, then selected supplies from her kit. She cleaned the area with an antiseptic towelette, then sprayed the pad. "That's an antibiotic, but it will also take some of the pain away."

After removing a needle from a pack that contained the most varied types of needles he'd ever seen, she tried to hook the thorn and pull it through, but it wouldn't budge.

Freeway gave a whimper, the first Wayne had ever heard from the big mongrel. Sophie looped her arms around the animal's neck and crooned to him. "Mom's real careful," she assured the dog. "She won't hurt you if she can help it."

The dog pressed his face into Sophie's shoulder and gave another soulful whimper.

"You big put-on," Wayne muttered, knowing he'd do the same thing with the mother given half a chance. Hell, she could operate on him without anesthesia if he could bury his face against her breasts while she did.

The heat swept through him at an alarming rate. Enough of those thoughts.

Carey studied the thorn a bit more, shook her head, then got out a scalpel. Wayne wrapped an arm around the dog's neck and held the paw in place for Carey. Lord, she really was equipped for surgery.

She sprayed the pad again, waited a few seconds while she pressed the sore place with her thumb, then quickly made a tiny incision in the pad. Freeway didn't move a muscle.

She soaked the drop of blood away with a gauze square, then plucked the thorn out with a pair of tweezers, pulling it all the way through the pad. Freeway gave a surprised yelp as the black bramble jerked free of the flesh. Carey sprayed the area again.

"I'm going to use a product that takes the place of skin for a while, since most animals chew any bandage off quicker than it took to put it on. This will resist saliva for a few hours, then you'll need to renew it. I'll give you the bottle."

She painted a liquid on the pad that hardened like fingernail polish, leaving a clear, shiny coat. "Okay, he's done. You can free him."

Freeway smelled his paw and gave an experimental lick or two at it. He sat up on his haunches and gave the paw a shake, then tried licking it again.

Sophie giggled. "It won't come off, silly."

"Here," Wayne said to the dog, "you deserve a treat after that ordeal." He poured the rest of his beer into a saucer he kept in the truck for the dog. Freeway lapped it up, while the kid laughed in delight and Carey tried to look disapproving, except for the laughter that kept leaping into her eyes.

"Can we eat now? I'm starved." Sophie turned to him. "Mom brought the best cake. We made it together and took it to Lorrie's house and had a big dinner Friday night. There were twenty-two people there, and a lot of them were kids like me. We played games after dark."

"That must have been fun," he commented, retrieving his lunch bag and thinking of the rather lonely bachelor gathering at the bunkhouse kitchen over the weekend. "I have a couple of sandwiches I can share."

"We have plenty," Carey said with her usual I-don't-take-a-thing-from-anyone attitude. She cleaned up her equipment, stored it neatly, gave him the bottle of stuff for Freeway's paw, then put the kit away.

She removed a bag of food from the backpack. His mouth watered when he spied fried chicken breasts, crisped potato skins, celery hearts stuffed with something that looked good, a plastic bowl of avocado dip and two big pieces of cake. Freeway went on the alert as soon as he got a whiff of the chicken.

"Down, boy," Wayne ordered.

"I'm Sophie," the kid announced. "What's your name?" She settled a napkin on her lap and took a loaded plastic plate from her mom.

"I'm called 'J.D.'"

Not exactly a lie, but not the whole truth. He found he didn't like lying to Carey, but it was hard to correct now that he'd lived with the name for so many months. Besides, he'd be on his way soon. As soon as he knew how little Jennifer McCallum was.

His half sister. And Clint Calloway, his half brother. And there were probably others, knowing his father as he had. Still, it was hard to think of leaving without telling them there were blood ties between them. It was true. Blood was thicker—

"Here." Carey held a plate out to him.

"I have a sandwich."

"You said we'd share," she reminded him.

She smiled in a sweet, natural way, as if they were friends, or could be if things went right. He wanted to do something—like kiss her hand in gratitude or something equally stupid. He took the plate.

She prepared one for herself. He offered her half of his roast beef sandwich. She accepted and took a seat on the opposite end of the tailgate. Sophie was sitting half in the truck to be close to Freeway.

Hearing a distinctive crunch and smacking noises behind him, he turned in time to see Sophie's chicken disappear down Freeway's gullet.

"Dammit—" He caught himself. "Dang blast it, Freeway. The ladies save your ornery life and you eat their lunch."

Sophie interceded. "I shared."

"She did," her mother agreed. "Sophie took a bite, then Freeway took a bite. Then Sophie took a bite and Freeway took a bite. He was very gentlemanly. Sophie gave him the rest when she didn't want any more."

Freeway sighed and laid his head on Sophie's leg below the plate. He gave her the most soulful stare Wayne had ever seen coming from a dog. Sophie was returning it.

"Love at first sight," Carey said, amusement flashing in her hazel eyes. The sun picked out specks of blue and brown and gold in them.

"Yeah, I know how he feels." He looked directly at her, reminding her of the instant attraction between them.

"Huh," she scoffed, but with a smile.

He bit into the chicken. "I must have died and gone to heaven. I haven't had anything this good since my mom—" He stopped, but it was too late to recall the words. Memories flooded his mind of times that had been good, when he and his family had been happy— or at least he had. He'd assumed the others were, too.

"Your mom?" Carey prompted.

"She used to like to try new dishes. Before she got sick and couldn't do much."

"Is she still alive?"

"No. She's been gone about twenty years."

"I'm sorry."

The simple sincerity almost unmanned him. He swallowed hard and waited for the tightening in his chest to dissolve. Damn but he was turning into a basket case today.

A new crunching had him looking back to the truck to see what Freeway was up to now. He and the kid were sharing the celery stick. Wayne shook his head. "Dogs don't eat celery, you dumb mutt."

"Freeway likes it," Sophie declared, springing to the defense of the big mongrel, who looked as if *he* had died and gone to doggie heaven.

Carey laughed aloud.

Wayne nearly fell off the tailgate. "A woman's laughter," he said softly. "It's a thing to warm a man's blood and go right to the heart."

"It doesn't take much to warm a man's blood." She gave him a sardonic grin when he frowned at her.

"Can Freeway and I go for a walk? We won't go far," Sophie promised, looking at her mom.

"If he feels like it," Carey agreed.

Sophie scooted to the end of the tailgate and hopped down. She didn't even have to call him. The dog jumped down right behind her and followed at her side, taking it easy on his sore paw. They walked down the dirt track.

"No farther than the big oak tree by that rock," Carey told her daughter. The girl nodded in understanding.

"She's a bright kid," he commented.

"Yes." A thoughtful frown settled on her face. "She's very loving and trusting."

"That worries you."

She sighed and leaned against the truck frame. "To the point of distraction. No matter how many times her father disappoints her, she still believes him the next time he says he's coming by or promises her an outing or a toy, all of which he promptly forgets."

"What do you do?"

"Nothing. Sophie explains to me and herself that he's busy…the way I am. Lorrie has been very good about including Sophie in her family life, so Sophie doesn't seem to mind that Jack and I aren't as dependable."

"You're a doctor."

"So I can be excused, but Jack isn't in medicine, so he can't?" She munched on a piece of chicken, then swallowed.

He frowned, not sure how she'd turned the tables on him, but she had. "You don't feel it entitles you to a bit more leeway than the rest of mankind?"

"My parents always said we're all people. All kinds of jobs are necessary to keep civilization going." She grinned. "Of course, I do feel a little above myself when a case turns around that others have given up on."

He rubbed his chin, remembering running into Sterling McCallum when he was talking to Reed Austin about some more beefs he'd found slaughtered in one of the back pastures four days ago. They figured Dale Carson was at it again, but who was behind the young man? That was the question.

"How's Jennifer McCallum?" he asked.

Carey's smile vanished, and he was sorry he'd brought the name up. Worry replaced the light in her eyes.

"She's ready for the marrow transplant."

"That's great. Calloway checked out okay, did he?" Wayne felt an immense relief. He could leave with a free conscience.

She shook her head. The sunlight glinted off the tousled curls in a carefree manner that belied the pity on her face. "The blood profile has to match on six basic points. His only hit four of them."

Wayne stopped with the last bite of chicken on the way to his mouth. "What do you mean?" he asked, already knowing the answer.

"He can't be a donor. Jessica insists on being checked. So does Sterling. And the entire hospital staff. But it's a long shot, without any family ties."

"But not impossible?"

"Nothing's impossible."

She sounded so grimly determined he knew if a miracle was needed, she'd find one.

"How long have you got?"

"As long as it takes." She sighed. "A few weeks, maybe months. We can give her blood transfusions for quite a while, but someday she'll get an infection or something…" Her voice trailed off.

She put her partly eaten lunch aside and sipped from the soda can, her gaze on the mountain peaks in the distance as if she were willing the miracle to happen right that moment. There was worry in the depths of her eyes.

"You can test me," he volunteered.

If he matched, he'd tell the truth. He could do like Clint, refuse to take any part of the Kincaid estate. Legally, he supposed it was all his, since he was the only legitimate heir, or would be if he made a court case of it. Which he wouldn't.

She gave him a thoughtful and slightly puzzled perusal. "That's kind of you."

She obviously didn't think he would have a snowball's chance of matching the six whatevers that had to fit. "I mean it," he assured her.

She met his eyes and held his gaze. The worry in her expression softened. "Why do you care?"

He looked away. "I've met the kid."

"To know her is to love her," Carey said softly, hearing the words he didn't say.

Wayne felt a hand touch his where it was clenched on the end of the tailgate. He turned his hand and linked his fingers with hers, enjoying the feel of her palm against his.

Like all doctors who had ever touched him—and there had been a hell of a lot of them when they'd gotten him back from 'Nam and worked on his wounds—her hands were very soft from all the scrubbing she did.

Slowly, giving her a chance to pull back, he brought his head closer to hers. Very gently, he kissed her, first her eyes until she closed them, then her lips until she opened them. He reached inside and stroked her tongue with his. She tasted of the soda.

He lifted his head. "I had a beer earlier. Sorry about that."

"I didn't notice."

Her frankness always surprised him. He grinned. "Then it was as good for you as it was for me?"

She gave him an exasperated grimace and shoved him away, then hopped off the tailgate. "I'm not going to tell you. Your ego is colossal already."

He chuckled and finished the chicken. Sophie had been right. It was the best he'd ever eaten.

"Sophie," Carey called. "Time to go."

"We haven't had the cake," he protested.

"You can have it. We have more at home."

"How about supper?" He knew he was pushing his luck, but she seemed to be feeling amiable toward him.

"Are you inviting me out to eat, or are you inviting yourself to eat at my house?" She was amused.

"Either. You and Sophie can come with me. I'll pick you up at seven."

She shook her head. "You can eat with us. Same time."

"Seven? I'll be there. At the Baxter cabin?"

"Yes."

He watched while she walked down the road to join her daughter. When they started back up the trail, he whistled. Freeway stopped and looked at him, then back at his new love. After a bit of heavy thinking, the animal finally turned and trotted back to the truck.

"You're fickle, fellow," Wayne said, rubbing the dog's ears. "What would Daisy think of this crush of yours?"

Daisy, their best cattle dog, had given birth to four puppies last month, thanks to Freeway's amorous attentions.

Wayne smiled. He knew one little girl who'd love to have one. And one mom who wouldn't. He chuckled.

Four

Wayne put the pickup in gear and headed back to ranch headquarters, but his mind strayed to the old Baxter cabin and the two females who'd spent a long weekend there. Today was Monday and not a holiday, so the doc had taken a day off to be with her daughter. In spite of the mother's guilt, the daughter seemed a well-balanced kid.

Carey was a warm, loving armful of woman. Any child would be lucky to have her for a parent. A man would be lucky to have her for a wife. The husband who'd let her go had been a fool.

The memory of her passionate response to him nearly had him running off the road. He sternly brought his attention back to the real world. A quarter mile down the dirt track, he noticed a mineral block in the pasture.

"What the hell?" he muttered.

They hadn't put out any new blocks, not in winter, and none out this way since last spring. By now, deer and other forest creatures should have finished it off.

He stopped the truck, the hairs on the back of his neck standing at attention. There were no tracks in the road in front of him. He got out and checked behind the pickup, walking on the dried grass and weeds along the verge.

His tires had obliterated the other vehicle's tracks, but he did find the imprint of a tire edge, then a few yards back, the place where a truck, its tires worn almost bald, had turned around.

Returning to the pickup, he grabbed a burlap bag and slipped through the barbed-wire strands. After retrieving the mineral block, he tossed it in the back and drove on to the ranch.

Rand Harding, the foreman, was in the ranch office when Wayne arrived. "Bad news," the foreman said as soon as he stepped inside the door.

"Yeah? Tell me about it," Wayne invited with a cynical smile.

"I just talked to Hargrove—"

"Was he out here?" Wayne interrupted.

Rand gave him a quizzical glance. "On the telephone. They've decided to shut down the ranch completely. As soon as it warms up and the cows have dropped their calves, the livestock will be sold at auction. Same goes for the equipment. I guess the ranch will go next."

"Did he say that?"

"No, but you don't even need to read between the lines to see it coming. I mean, what else are they going to do? The ranch needs an income to pay the taxes. Nobody wants to work here because of the so-called Kincaid curse." He sighed despondently. "Hargrove says they've had an offer."

For a second, Wayne felt something hot and heavy clench at his insides. He forced himself to relax. Hell, this was what he wanted. Let the ranch go. In a few years it would be known as the old Kincaid place the same as the Baxter ranch.

End of an era.

"Who from?"

"I don't know. He didn't say."

Rand tapped the end of a pencil on the scarred ranch desk. The younger man's eyes were dark. His shoulders slumped. Wayne realized the foreman would be out of a job with the shutdown of the ranch. So would he.

Maybe he'd head for Denver. A friend from the military had urged him to join his private-detective agency for years. The two had been paired up in the hospital for a brief spell while recovering from their wounds. They'd remained in contact over the years. Yeah, maybe it was time to be moving on.

As soon as he knew Jennifer was going to be okay. Things weren't looking good on that front.

He swallowed hard to clear his throat before he spoke again. "Did you take a block of mineral salt out to section eight over near the Baxter ridge?"

"No. It's too early. Besides, we probably won't be moving any cattle out this year if what Hargrove says is true about closing down completely, so we won't be doing anything in the back pastures."

"That's what I thought. Odd, though. I found a brand-new block out there. I brought it in with me. Thought I might have the sheriff check it out."

Rand stared at him, then set his jaw angrily. "I'd like to find the bastard who's doing this."

"So would I. If I could find Dale and have five minutes alone with him, I think we'd have the answer."

"Yeah. You think it would do any good to talk to McCallum and see if we can't make it another year before we throw in the towel? The deputy has the final say."

"It wouldn't hurt to ask."

"That's what I thought. I, mmm, wondered if you'd do it." At Wayne's sharp glance, he hurried on. "You seem to be on pretty easy terms with him. And you're closer in age."

The foreman grinned as he added the last. The other ranch hands, what few there were, called Wayne "Gramps." He was ten to twenty years older than the rest of them.

And felt every damn one of those years. He pushed a grin on his face and nodded. "Reckon I can do that."

He needed to see Sterling and his wife anyway. Confession time was drawing closer unless Carey had found a donor for Jennifer.

He wondered what the doc's reaction would be. Shock. Disbelief. Anger. About half the county would probably feel the same. Including Ethan, assuming Kate hadn't already said something to him. Then there was Carey and McCallum and his wife. They would have to be told, too.

Then, when he'd done all he could for the kid, he'd be out of Whitehorn. For good.

Carey waved a piece of newspaper toward the door. She muttered several nasty phrases. "Go outside, Sophie, until I get the smoke cleared out."

Her daughter skipped out of the cabin and settled on the steps. Carey wondered where the wind was when she needed it. She heard a truck stop outside and went to join her daughter on the porch. She glanced at her watch.

"You're early," she called to J.D. "It's only six."

"Freeway here couldn't wait," he explained.

The dog jumped out of the truck and made a beeline for Sophie, who was already giggling and holding her arms open. They rushed at each other like long-lost lovers. The dog licked the girl all over her face.

Carey felt a hitch in the vicinity of her heart. Ah, to be that young and find happiness so easily. She looked at J.D., standing at the bottom of the steps, a strangely gentle smile on his lips as he watched the child and his dog.

"Looks like we need the fire department," he remarked.

He was dressed in jeans and boots as usual, but he'd put on a white shirt, sleeves rolled back on his forearms, in place of the work shirt he'd worn earlier. His hair appeared damp.

"That blasted stove delights in driving me crazy. It won't light. And yes, I have the flue open," she said before he could make one of those superior-male remarks.

He grinned and ambled inside with her. He put a hand on the old-fashioned potbellied stove as if taking its temperature. "Cold," he said.

"I noticed," she informed him sarcastically. "That's why I was trying to light the blasted thing. We need some heat. I don't know why I let Sophie talk me into spending the night out here. It's much too early for camping in this drafty place."

"It's peaceful," he said, as if that explained it all.

He picked up the newspaper she'd used as a fan to dispel the smoke and tore off a section, then made a twist out of it. He lit the twist and stuck it inside the stove and toward the opening to the stovepipe.

The wisp of smoke from the burning paper swirled for a couple of seconds while the flame fluttered, then both flame and smoke straightened and went up the pipe. He then laid the twist on her little pile of smol-dering paper and kindling. The fire caught and the smoke in the room whisked into the stove on the draft.

She glared at him.

He chuckled while he wiped smudges of soot off his hand with a handkerchief. "The air in the stovepipe was cold. That's why it couldn't draw. It needed a little direct flame to heat things up and get the air to moving."

"Oh."

"There are some things you don't know, Doc."

He gave her a sexy, oblique glance that had her heart

diving to her toes and making her want to tap-dance. She frowned, irritated at herself and her reaction to this audacious cowboy. "I'm sure you've picked up lots of tidbits while drifting around the world."

"Yeah," he agreed in a harder tone. "It teaches a man a thing or two—like to watch out for smart-mouthed women."

A giggle interrupted them before the quarrel, if that's what it was, picked up steam. Sophie came in with Freeway and closed the door, shutting out the cold night air.

"Mom doesn't like it when you talk back," she advised J.D. "When are we going to eat?"

"Soon. Now that I can see through the smoke." Her smile was a peace offering. "Thanks for clearing the air."

Sophie started a game of tug-of-war with Freeway, using one of Carey's socks. The dog growled playfully, while the girl laughed in delight as they romped around the table.

J.D. waved her thanks aside. "You know, this cabin could be fixed up pretty quick if you wanted to use it for weekend getaways on a regular basis. An extra room could be added on the back side. The door could be cut where this window is. A porch around three sides would give you a shady place to sit no matter where the sun is."

"That sounds nice. I'll have to find a handyman. When I have time," she added.

"I could do it."

She glanced at him in surprise. His expression was chagrined, as if he were angry with himself for volunteering, then it was gone, his face once more cast in granite.

"I'm sure you'll be much too busy at the ranch to come over here and work," she murmured, excusing him.

He hesitated before answering. "Right. I could draw you a plan, though."

"Do you know how?"

He gave a mock frown at her doubting tone. "I worked in construction for a while, putting up expensive cabins in the mountains for the yuppies. I learned a thing or two."

"I'll bet you did."

His slow grin picked up the corners of his sensual mouth. "You do have a wicked tongue. Do you use it for anything but lashing a man's hide off?"

"Sometimes." Meeting his gaze, she realized she was flirting with him. The idea amazed her. She, Carey Hall, voted the most dedicated to her goals by her high-school class, flirting?

Sophie and Freeway flopped on the rug in front of the stove, which was now putting out a generous amount of heat. He tended the fire, then reached into his pocket and pulled out a short reed.

"I found this whistle today." He handed it to Sophie.

She blew through it. "This isn't a whistle," she said, disappointed in her new friend.

"It isn't? Let me look at it." He peered at the reed. "Well, shucks, it doesn't have enough holes."

He pulled out a knife and, with the tip of a blade, drilled three small holes along the reed. He stuck his finger over the bottom hole, then blew into the other end.

A light note filled the room. Using his fingers to cover one, then another of the holes, he made different sounds so that the effect was like that of wind chimes, an oddly pleasing blend of airy tones that almost sounded like a melody. Sophie's eyes rounded with pleasure.

"Oh, let me try," she cried.

J.D. handed over the whistle.

Carey was delighted when Sophie also made the reed flute sing. She realized J.D. had shown her daughter how a flute was made and how something as simple as a reed could make beautiful music, all without a word of instruction.

She turned on the two-burner hot plate that had come with the old cabin and whipped up the batter for hoecakes with cornmeal, milk and an egg. Using a flat iron skillet, she ladled the batter out pancake-fashion to cook. She dumped barbecued beans and beef, which she'd made and brought with them, into a pan and set it to heating on the other burner.

"That was kind of you," she murmured when J.D. came over and watched.

"I can be kind."

His gravelly voice stroked her like rough velvet, and she knew she was in danger of being enchanted by this mysterious drifter. She let herself inhale the masculine aroma of soap and shampoo and aftershave lotion and thought of losing herself in his arms…

And when he was gone? What of enchantment then?

The stern voice of practicality burst her pretty daydream. She had Sophie to think of. A drifter would do her child no good. Children trusted so readily. He would win the child's love, then break her heart when he left.

He traced the frown line between her eyes with a finger. "Lighten up, Carey. The world won't come to an end, no matter what happens or doesn't happen between us."

"No, it won't," she agreed briskly, letting her irritation show. She flipped the hoecakes on the flat skillet, let them brown and took them up. Then she ladled on the next batch and stirred the pot. "Sophie, time to set the table. Wash up first."

The girl gave one last pat to Freeway, then washed her hands in a basin before standing on tiptoe to retrieve plates from shelves on the wall. She put out forks and napkins for the three of them.

Carey was aware of J.D. watching the activity. She gave him a questioning glance as she set the platter of hoecakes on the table, then poured up the beans and beef in a bowl.

"Springwater okay?" she asked, holding up a glass.

"Fine."

He played the gallant, refusing to sit until they did, then holding their chairs for them. Actually, there were only two chairs. Sophie sat on a stool made from a section of log. He watched as Carey put a hoecake on Sophie's plate, then spooned the beans-and-beef mixture over it.

"I was wondering how you ate those." He helped himself to a double stack of bread and barbecue.

"Do you know why they're called 'hoecakes'?" Sophie demanded.

"No, why?"

"Farmers used to cook them on a hoe over the fire." She laughed in delight when he clasped a hand to his chest and looked as if he might fall off the chair in amazement. "My granddad and I tried it once when he lived in town, but the hoecake caught on fire."

"Sounds as if your granddad was a fun guy."

"Yes," she said in the manner of kids who take it for granted that everyone has wonderful grandparents.

Later, the three of them had canned peaches with the rest of the cake and played Go Fish. After the game, Sophie changed into flannel pajamas with feet and fell asleep on the floor in front of the stove, her arm around Freeway's neck, his chin resting on her shoulder.

"Norman Rockwell could do justice to that scene," Carey said, pointing to the two.

"Yes."

She was aware that his eyes didn't leave her. She put on a pot of coffee, then started on the dishes. He dried and put the dishes on the shelf.

"You're handy to have around," she teased.

"In more ways than one."

The smoldering laugher in his eyes invited her to relax and enjoy all he was offering. She wiped the wooden counter next to the hot plate and hung up the dishcloth.

"Should she be in bed?" he asked, nodding to Sophie.
"Yes."

He lifted the girl into his arms and took her to the bunk on the far side of the cabin. She settled into her sleeping bag without a sound. After adding another log to the stove, he resumed his seat.

Carey poured the coffee and brought the mugs to the table. "It's decaffeinated," she said for no reason except to fill the silence. His gentleness with Sophie only added to her confusion about him.

He caught her hand when she would have moved away. With a little tug, he pulled her into his lap.

She glanced over her shoulder to where her daughter slept peacefully. "Don't."

"We're not going to do anything in a one-room cabin with a dog and a kid present," he murmured, pressing his face against her neck and inhaling deeply. "Well, maybe a little quiet necking. Ah, the scent of a woman."

Chills ran helter-skelter over her while his breath caressed her throat. His hands—mmm, those long, graceful fingers—rubbed her back and along the muscles of her shoulders, massaging and soothing away the tightness she'd lived with all week.

She felt air in the vee between her breasts. Looking down, she saw him unfasten the next button of her plaid woodcutter's shirt. He kissed the dip between her breasts, then flicked his tongue there, leaving a cool spot on her skin, while heat erupted deep within and quickly spread to every part of her.

"Pretty," he said, gazing at the light-green bra with its floral motif of spring flowers. "So the doc has a soft side."

"It was part of a Christmas set from my mom," Carey said defensively.

His hand went to the snap on her jeans. "You mean, there's more?" Devilish laughter leaped into his eyes, but he made no move to check further.

She wondered if she would have the energy to stop him if he tried. The lazy amusement in his voice almost did her in. His hands slipped under her loose shirt and continued their relaxing massage. Her thoughts blurred as he tilted his head to one side and covered her mouth with his.

They kissed for a long time, his hands inside her shirt, hers finding his buttons and doing the same to him. Once he caught her hands and held them away from his body, although his lips didn't leave hers. She moaned in protest.

At last, he pressed her face to his chest and held her there, his fingers stroking through her hair while their blood cooled from sizzle to normal.

"Ah, gal," he whispered, "but you'd make a saint forget his promises."

"What promises?" she murmured, sleepy now that the passion had dissipated.

"To never settle in one place too long."

He stood and set her on her feet, his eyes shaded by thoughts she couldn't read.

"You're going to have to put the past behind you someday," she told him.

His expression hardened. "I have."

"Not yet you haven't."

"Is this a free consultation, Doc?" he drawled, his way of telling her she was stepping across his bounds.

"Yes." She pulled the open sides of her shirt across her breasts and held the ends in place with her arms folded over her chest.

He buttoned his shirt, then snapped his fingers. Freeway thumped his tail, but didn't raise his head.

"Come on, you mangy mutt, it's time to leave."

Freeway sighed and closed his eyes.

J.D. looked resigned. "He can stay the night. Throw him out tomorrow when you leave. He'll head back for the ranch."

She hesitated, not sure she even wanted his dog in the cabin. "Okay."

He stopped at the door, then slipped an arm around her and pulled her against him, giving her a hard, soul-stirring kiss. "There, that's one for the road."

And one to dream on, she thought later, nestled into her sleeping bag on the other hard bunk. For a few heartbeats, she let herself think about snuggling up to a tough male body, then she put the thought aside.

Marriage and medicine didn't mix. She'd learned that the hard way. No more dreams of tomorrow. If she and J.D. shared anything, it would be for the moment.

When he was gone, she'd be alone again.

The wind picked up and whistled around the cabin, reminding her of the notes from a reed flute. It was the loneliest sound.

She finally went to sleep, and didn't wake until a cold

nose touched her cheek at dawn the next morning. She pushed it away. Freeway huffed in her ear. Sitting upright, Carey realized where she was. She patted the dog's head and got up to let him out. He bounded across the lawn and loped down the dirt road. She realized he was going home.

When Sophie awoke, the first thing she wanted was the dog. "Where's Freeway?" she demanded, sitting up, instantly wide-awake and ready for play.

"I think he headed for the ranch. He probably wanted his breakfast and knew we didn't have anything for him. He gave you a goodbye kiss."

"He did?"

"Uh-huh. Right on your nose."

It was the kind of fib she'd told her daughter for years about her father when he didn't show up. She'd say he had called and would catch her next weekend. Once she'd even sent the child a card and pretended it was from him, but she'd felt so guilty for the lie that she hadn't done it again. She'd suggested to Jack that he might write to make sure Sophie didn't forget him. That had struck his vanity, and he actually remembered to do it a couple of times a year.

Sophie laughed, rubbed her nose and was happy.

"Time to get dressed. You have school and I have to get to the office at nine this morning."

"That's late," Sophie said with a child's knowledge of adult ways.

"Yes. I've decided to start my workday a little later so I can get you off to school before I leave. Next year when you go to first grade, you can ride the bus to Lorrie's house so she won't have to come get you."

"Okay." Sophie pulled off her pajamas and dressed.

The all-too-ready tears rushed to Carey's eyes. She was so lucky to have this easygoing child.

She glanced out the window to where J.D.'s pickup had been parked. She had her work, her daughter, her house in town and now a ranch—well, sort of. She didn't need anything else, no matter how nice it had felt to cuddle in J.D.'s arms and be kissed right to heaven.

Five

"Yo, Cade."

Wayne stopped and waited for the young cop to come down the courthouse steps and join him on the sidewalk.

"Your hunch was right," Reed Austin said. "The mineral block was laced with poison. It would have been slow death for any animal that licked it."

"Arsenic?" Wayne knew it had a cumulative effect, the poison lurking in the body until enough had built up to kill.

Reed shook his head. "It was something the crime lab hadn't run into before. A muscle relaxer that isn't used because of the danger. I don't have a clue where anyone would get the stuff. It isn't on the market."

Wayne considered this information, one part of him going cold with fury. If he could get hold of Dale Carson for just five minutes—

"You look as if you're contemplating murder," Reed remarked, a warning in his tone.

"Nah. Maybe a little friendly persuasion on a couple of guys." He rubbed his chin and tried to think. Something was niggling at the back of his mind. "A muscle relaxer, huh? Sure seems odd to use something like that."

"It's hard to detect. One of the new lab guys thought of checking for a relaxant because of the recent death of a kid who got in his parents' medicine cabinet and tried one."

Wayne was reminded of Jenny and her illness. He had a sense of time speeding by faster and faster. He needed to talk to Kate and Ethan and others before it ran out.

"I don't suppose they could detect fingerprints on the block, could they?"

Reed shook his head. "I've got an appointment with the city attorney. It seems we're being sued for false arrest. A cop can't win for losing." His grin was cynical as he headed for his car.

Wayne started for his truck. He was going to stop by the McCallum house. He wanted to talk to Sterling about the ranch. Hell, he wanted to talk him out of selling. For some stupid reason, it had become important to him.

Down the street, he saw Janie Carson come out of one of the department stores, several packages in her arms. He wondered, not for the first time, if she knew where her brother was hiding. Could he find out?

For a second, his conscience bothered him, then he grimly stalked along the sidewalk. Some things were more important than personal ethics. Besides, he hated to see whoever was trying to ruin the ranch succeed.

"Hey, Janie, going to work?" he asked, striding up to her with a falsely cheerful smile.

She blinked at him as if not quite sure he was talking to her. "No, taking my packages to my car."

"Here, let me help." He took the largest bags from her and swung into step beside her. "Nice day, huh?"

It was. The temperature was in the forties. The sun was shining, the air was clear and the sky a robin's-egg blue. Some store windows were decorated with hearts and red and white streamers for Valentine's Day, still a month away. He was reminded of a gift he had to take care of.

Adjusting his step to hers, he walked with Janie to her car, which was located on the street next to the city park. He chatted with her about her job and teased her about buying valentines for all the guys in town.

She tossed her head and gave him sassy answers and flirted with him outrageously. His smile became a real one as he enjoyed her performance. She was good with her eyes, flashing him under-the-lashes glances as she told of a humorous incident while shopping.

She locked her packages in the trunk of her compact car.

"How about a coffee?" she suggested. "We could drink it here in the park."

A pinch of guilt took hold of him. He shook it off.

After all, he was on important business, even if he was going about it in an underhanded fashion. "Sure."

He went with her to the café and paid for the two coffees. He grinned. "We're getting citified here in the sticks, aren't we? Gourmet coffee, bagels and all that."

She laughed, a tinkling, teasing, girl's laughter, wrinkled her pert nose at him and pushed her lips into a pouty expression that begged to be kissed. She was as subtle as one of Freeway's pups, wriggling all over itself wanting to be petted.

For an instant, he was reminded of Kate and him, back when they'd both been eighteen and in love, and life had seemed theirs for the taking. God, what a long time past that had been.

He dusted off one of the park benches and invited her to sit beside him. The sun felt good on his back as they sat facing the street. Their shoulders touched as Janie snuggled closer. He hoped Reed Austin didn't see them.

Wayne suspected the cop was more than half in love with Janie. If she was smart, she'd snap the young man up. She'd have a secure future with Reed, which was a lot more than any woman would get from him.

It was time to be moving on. He could feel it in his bones, in every breath he breathed. Yet this place of his birth was growing on him. Sometimes he remembered only what was good about living here....

"How are things on the ranch?" Janie asked.

Ah, the perfect lead-in. "Not so good. McCallum has ordered it closed down. It would be a shame to lose his daughter's inheritance, especially now when she might need the money for her treatment. I understand it's expensive."

He sat silently, letting the words soak in.

Janie stared into the middle distance, her young face pensive and troubled. She swallowed, then licked her lips.

He held his breath, sure she was going to tell him where the young man was hiding. Maybe she knew who Dale was in cahoots with, too. He leaned closer, taking on a confidential air, his lips close to her ear.

"Janie," he murmured, "we need help. If you know anything that would—" He broke off as he stared into eyes so cold they would have frosted a store window at twenty paces.

Carey Hall averted her gaze and strode on down the sidewalk, her head high as she pretended not to see him sitting there with Janie, making out with the impressionable youngster as he tried to pry information out of her.

"Hell," he said.

Janie jerked as if startled out of a trance. "What?"

"Nothing." He sighed and glanced at his watch. "I have to go. I have an appointment."

Janie now wore a frown. He could see she didn't think much of him at the moment. He didn't think much of himself.

"Were you using me to make Dr. Hall jealous?" she demanded, her hands on her cup as if she might throw the hot coffee in his face.

"Yeah," he said.

Janie missed the ironic overtone. "I think you're a beast." She flounced off.

He finished off the coffee and tossed the cup toward the trash bin. Missed. He picked it up and slam-dunked it into the bin. So far his day had been a perfect zero, and it was now time for his meeting with the deputy.

Five minutes later, he stopped in front of the McCallum house. He climbed out, his heart kicking up a bit when he saw Carey's ute in the drive.

He wondered if she'd brought good news. Maybe they'd found a donor for Jenny. She hadn't told him where to go or when to come in for testing. That was something he needed to ask about. Maybe she didn't need him. Maybe someone else matched, and he could leave.

Sterling answered his knock. "Come on in. We're nearly finished." He led the way into the living room.

Jessica smiled and spoke in her usual manner. Jennifer played on the floor in front of the fire with a doll and tea set. The doc nodded, but didn't speak.

He noticed Jessica's eyes were red. As if she'd cried shortly before his arrival. The deputy was as grim as death. Carey, too, was blinking her eyes suspiciously.

"I, uh, wanted to talk to you about the ranch. The foreman asked me to stop by." He felt awkward, as if he, the outsider, had intruded on a family scene. "Should I come by later?"

"No," Jessica answered. "It's all right. I was just taking Jenny to the bedroom for her nap. If that's all?"

She looked at Carey, who nodded, then she swept the child into her arms and hurried out. The little girl was thin, and as pale as a mist. Her shiny, bouncy curls were gone. Tufts of colorless hair wafted around her face.

Something clenched hard and achy in his chest. He listened to the kid tell her mom about her tea party until a door closed down the hall, shutting off the childish treble.

"What is it?" he asked, looking from one to the other.

Sterling didn't answer.

Carey spread her hands in a helpless gesture. "Sterling and Jessica don't match Jennifer's blood profile. They can't be donors. We've tested a full dozen people now. It's like looking for the proverbial needle in the haystack."

"You haven't tested me. I said I'd volunteer. Where do I go?"

She gave him a doubtful perusal. "There probably isn't any need—"

"I said, I'll do it," he snapped, angry with her for closing him out, with himself for trying a cheap trick with Janie, angry with the whole damn situation.

He saw her and Sterling exchange glances, then she nodded. "All right. Can you report to the hospital tomorrow around noon?"

"Yes."

"Fine." She stood. "I'll let you know the moment we find anything," she said to Sterling, who jerked his head once in understanding.

After she left, the emptiness of the room closed in around the two men. Wayne pondered this for a moment. With the women gone, life seemed diminished somehow. Odd, that.

"I wanted to talk to you about the ranch. Did Reed tell you about the mineral block I found?" he asked.

For the next half hour, he and the deputy discussed the Kincaid place that was Jennifer's heritage. If the kid died, McCallum and his wife would inherit the ranch. Not that they wanted it. He could tell that.

"I have some ideas about the place," he started, then decided it wasn't the time. "Once we get the problem of the Kincaid curse settled."

Sterling snorted. "You believe in curses?"

"I believe in people trying to make others believe in them. I never heard of a cow dying of fright from seeing a ghost, and no ghost planted that poison."

"Right."

He discussed the ranch for another fifteen minutes. "There's something niggling in the back of my mind. Some clue I'm missing or maybe something I've forgot—" He stopped before he gave his past away. "It'll come to me."

"I hope it does before you get a bullet in the head. We could use some help on this case."

Wayne smiled at Sterling's gallows humor and got up to go. "So do I."

He drove back to the ranch, his thoughts on the days ahead. He'd nearly given his identity away several times recently. He would have to confess and explain his past actions soon.

Carey closed the file and slid it into its slot at the nurses' station. "If J. D. Cade comes in, would you page me?"

"Sure," Annie said, flipping her red braid over her shoulder and out of the way while she painted clear nail polish across the run in her stocking. She blew on the polish, then pulled her skirt down over the run. "Where will you be?"

"In the cafeteria. I'll eat lunch here before heading back to the office."

As she walked down the corridor, she realized she'd said "if," not "when." She didn't expect him to show up. Her senses were keen where he was concerned. She instinctively knew he was restless. He'd be gone soon.

The thought dampened her already gloomy spirits, which matched the weather. It was raining hard. The rain would probably turn to sleet by night. She had a long day ahead of her and would be out on the icy roads after dark.

Just as she reached the cafeteria line, she heard her name over the page. She turned and retraced her steps along the hall, then went into the reception area. J.D. was there, talking to Sara, the records clerk, who was charmingly, shyly, flustered by his presence.

Carey smiled ironically. Flustered wasn't half of what she felt around him. She was fast losing her fight to avoid him and stay out of his arms. She wanted him. It was that simple. And that complicated.

With a resigned sigh, she went forward. "So you came."

"I said I would," he said in that wonderful voice that was like rough velvet.

Her breasts beaded when his sultry blue gaze swept over her. She was dressed in black wool slacks and a green sweater under her surgical smock, which was open down the front. He paused at the evidence of her arousal. A slow smile kicked up the corners of his mouth.

She made a threatening face at him when Sara bent over her charts and pretended not to see the byplay between them. He grinned openly.

"The lab is this way." She strode off with a determined air of brisk efficiency without waiting to see if he came along or not.

His chuckle assured her he was right behind her. "Will this take long?"

"No." Her short reply raised the sandy eyebrows of the lab technician, who had started work there the same day she'd opened her office.

"I'll need you to fill out this form," Bill, the technician, told J.D., handing over the clipboard. "Sit here."

She noticed J.D. hesitate as he held the pen over the first line. He glanced up and met her eyes. A prickling sensation attacked her scalp. She had the strangest feeling he was going to tell her something.

But he didn't. He quickly wrote in the information on the standard form and handed the clipboard back to Bill.

She moved over to the window and gathered her composure around her as if it were a cloak she'd accidentally dropped.

Bill glanced at the form. "I have to know your full name. What do the *J* and *D* stand for?"

"That's it," J.D. said. "Nothing else."

"Oh. Okay. I'll add 'initials only' at the end of the line." He showed the cowboy what he'd done.

The technician quickly performed the procedure, filling the vials of blood necessary for the tests that would determine if J. D. Cade could be used as a bone marrow donor for Jennifer McCallum.

Carey suddenly hoped that he could. She wanted it desperately, as if her own life were at stake. The oddest thing was she wanted it for him. He didn't know it, but he had a need to be needed.

She didn't know how she knew that, but there it was. She was as positive of it as she was that the sun was still shining behind the layer of black clouds that hovered over Whitehorn and most of southern Montana.

"Okay, we're done," Bill said.

She faced the room again. Bill stuck a strip bandage over J.D.'s arm, then left the room with the vials of blood in a metal pan. They would be on their way to the state lab within the hour.

"How long before you'll know?" J.D. asked.

"We'll have the results in a week," she told him.

"A week," he repeated.

She would almost swear he sounded like a man who'd gotten a last-minute reprieve from the governor.

Reprieve from what?

That was the question. There was something going on that she didn't understand, but she was aware of the vibes in the air. It wasn't just sexual tension between her and him, either, but something more....

"Have you had lunch?" she asked.

"No. You paying, Doc?" He gave her an amused look while he rolled down his sleeve and buttoned the cuff.

"Yes."

"All right." He took her arm. "Is this a date?"

"You wish," she scoffed, automatically playing the role she'd adopted with him.

Once seated with their food in the cafeteria, she gazed at him, puzzled. "Something is different. What?"

"I don't know." He picked up his hamburger.

"Yes, you do. You're not saying." Again, she didn't know how she knew that, but she did. Anger brewed in her at his reticence. "I'll find out."

He gazed at her a long minute, then shook his head as if he didn't know what she was talking about.

But he did. She felt it in her bones.

Six

"Say that again." Carey tossed her reading glasses on the desk and clutched the telephone cord.

"You've got a donor," Dr. Holt, head of the testing lab informed her, a smile in his voice. "You should have heard the cheer that went up in the lab when I told them."

"Who? Which one?" She'd sent in three samples of blood for testing.

"J. D. Cade. I'll get the report in the mail in the morning, but I thought you'd like to know tonight."

"Yes. God, yes. Thanks so much for calling. Oh, any chance you could fax the report now. I want it in hand so I can look at it." She laughed at her eagerness.

Dr. Holt chuckled, too. "Sure thing. Good night."

"Good night, and thanks again for calling." She hung

up and collapsed into the chair behind her desk. A donor. J.D. She couldn't believe it. She pressed the heels of her hands against her eyes and rubbed the sting of tears away.

She reached for the telephone again, anxious to tell Jessica and Sterling. And to call J.D.

No. Not until she got the official report. Better to have it in hand and look it over herself before getting everyone all excited. Just in case.

J.D. He was the donor. In addition to his blood, she'd sent in two more samples with the same blood type as Jenny's, but until this moment, she hadn't let herself hope at all.

The telephone connected to the fax machine rang. In a few seconds, it began clacking, then spit out the report. She grabbed the pages and skimmed the entire report. A match on all six counts, verified and signed off by Dr. Holt himself. It was official. She grabbed the phone and called the ranch.

The foreman answered. "J.D.? He ran into town to pick up a part we'd ordered over at the machine shop. You want me to tell him you called?"

"Yes. This is Carey Hall. Have him call me. I'm at the office, but I'm leaving in about five minutes. I'll be at home the rest of the evening."

As soon as she confirmed he would go through with it, she'd call the McCallums. Or maybe she should wait for tomorrow. They wouldn't sleep a wink tonight.

Taking a deep breath, she composed herself and gathered her purse, checked that she had her keys and searched her pockets for the new pair of gloves she'd bought just the other day.

The day she'd seen J.D. in the park with Janie, the waitress from the Hip Hop Café.

Even that little scene couldn't detract from the relief she felt upon finding hope for Jenny. His private life was none of her business. She was interested in him strictly for medical reasons. With this firmly in mind, she headed for the side door.

The front bell rang in the outer office. She hesitated. At this hour, it was most likely an emergency. She turned back, tossed her things into a chair and went to the front of the Victorian building she shared with Kane Hunter.

"J.D.," she said stupidly after she flipped the dead bolt and opened the door.

He stood with his hat in his hand. Rain glistened on the poncho he wore over his shearling jacket. "Harding left word at the shop that you were trying to get hold of me."

"Yes." She stood aside when he entered. The door closed with a soft click, as if it punctuated the word.

He stripped out of the poncho and hung it and his dark-gray Stetson on a peg. "You need to do more tests?" he asked, facing her.

She shook her head. The tears, the foolish, foolish tears, crowded her throat so she couldn't speak.

He bent slightly and peered into her eyes. "What is it? Bad news? I'm not a match," he concluded.

"No, no. I mean, yes. Yes, you are. That's why I was calling. You're a perfect match. All six factors. I'm so glad. Jessica and Sterling… You will do it, won't you? You'll be the donor?" She stared at him anxiously.

"Of course. I said I would."

She laughed. Somehow it turned into a sob. She pressed a hand over her mouth, completely at odds with herself. She was a doctor. She was supposed to be cool and calm at all costs. But she didn't feel that way at all.

"Hey, now," he murmured, touching the side of her face.

She went to him then. She stepped forward. Or maybe he did. She felt his body heat as his arms slipped around her. It was like walking into a warm room. Like coming home.

He tried to hold her, to comfort her, but that wasn't enough. It wasn't what she wanted. She needed more. She closed her fists on his jacket lapels and pressed upward.

"Woman?" he questioned.

"Yes," she said. "Yes, oh, yes."

His arms stiffened, then his muscles gave a mighty flex against her breasts. The light was blotted out as his mouth came down on hers. His lips were soft, yet hard. His tongue stroked her lips. She opened and invited him inside.

The hunger grabbed her. Need flashed into flame. It was a roar in her head, drowning other sounds such as caution or the voice of reason. She clung to him, writhed against him and demanded a like passion from him.

"Hold on," he said. He tried to move away.

Desperation poured through her like a flood of champagne. "No."

His hands slipped between them. "Just let me get my coat off."

As soon as he got it open, she slid her hands inside and over his lean torso. The jacket hit the floor with a muted plop. He reached under her cardigan and caressed her back with his wonderful hands.

It still wasn't enough.

She tugged at his shirt, wanting it gone. "I want to touch you," she said. "Now. Take it off. Hurry."

"You, too. Take your sweater off."

It was crazy. Insane. Mindless. She knew all that and she didn't care. The worry, the tension, the wanting and never having—all came together in this one moment of fire and lust and longing.

"This way," she said. She led him into her office. She threw her cardigan on the chair with her purse and kicked her shoes off.

He closed the blinds, shutting out the street light and the shadows cast by the pouring rain. She removed her slacks and her blouse. He turned on the desk lamp, then took off his shirt and draped it across the lamp, filtering the light to a glow that matched the one inside her.

"Hurry," she said impatiently when he stood watching her. Panic ate at her, as if they would both disappear if she paused.

He sat on the sofa and removed his boots. When the rest of her clothing joined those on her desk chair, she turned to him. With quick, efficient movements, she stripped him of his jeans. He got his shirt off before she could help there.

He wore a dark-blue thermal T-shirt and white briefs. There were scars. She saw them, knew what they were, but there was no time to dwell on that just then.

She crashed into his arms, fiery with needs that were boundless and out of control. Sounds like those of a wounded animal needing succor slipped from her throat, as she sought the haven of his mouth with hers.

He took her weight easily, holding her as tightly as she held him. His lips and tongue moved with hers, answering her kiss and letting her set the mad, furious pace.

At some point, he gathered her up, lifting her feet from the floor, and pivoted a quarter turn. The short velvet nap of the sofa caressed her back. He laid a pillow behind her head and gently pushed her backward until she lay supine. She caught his hand.

He rubbed his thumb along her wrist while he gazed at her, his eyes roaming from one point to another, pausing, then moving on. "You're a beautiful woman, Carey Hall."

For a few seconds, she basked in the admiration, but it wasn't enough. She wanted him. Now.

When she tugged on his hand, he settled his long, lean body over hers. Their legs meshed as if they'd done this a thousand times. Thighs, bellies, chests, all the warm living flesh of their separate bodies came together. A bit of shifting, the settling of part of his weight on his arms, and they fit perfectly.

"Come to me."

"Carey, honey, I didn't bring anything," he said, humor in his voice. "You got any samples we can try."

"I'm on the pill. A doctor's life is too hectic—" She stopped abruptly and stared up at him.

He smiled in that slow, easy way he had. "Then we're all right. I've always been careful." He touched her temple, tracing a vein there. "I'll be careful with you."

But she didn't want careful. She wanted now. She wanted frantic and hot. She wanted to reap the whirlwind of passion that she'd denied for months. Since she'd met this blue-eyed stranger with his slow smile and wonderful hands, she'd wanted this. With him.

"Oh," she murmured when he stroked her just so.

"This is going to be good," he promised.

She found out how good. As in mind-blowing. As in out of control. As in wild and furious and fast. His hands were everywhere. His mouth followed, dropping kisses over her the way the rain fell upon the land, drenching her in delight.

Sometimes she sighed. She sobbed. When he finally came to her, she cried out at the hot, wet joining, the heated thrust of his flesh on hers, the wonderful, sweaty, slippery feel of his skin against hers. The world condensed to a point and disappeared.

She tossed her head. She struggled as if they fought. He held her secure, his weight keeping her grounded. She clung to him as the world heaved under her. She would have screamed, but he had locked his mouth on hers and refused to let go.

The release was explosive.

She went utterly still as colors flew against her closed eyelids—reds and brilliant yellows, vibrant green and a blue so perfectly beautiful it would have made the ocean pale by comparison.

At that moment, she felt him throb heavily in her. He lay still, then moved again, slowly, bringing them back from that wild passionate place they'd visited. The colors went to pastel, then blinked out. She opened her eyes.

He watched her without speaking. Perspiration beaded his face. Hers, too. She sighed shakily, totally drained but not exactly content. For once in her life, she didn't know what to do next.

His breath caressed her neck. With an easy movement, he turned them so that she lay snug between his body and the back of the sofa. He coaxed her leg over his. They remained locked together.

"I—"

"Rest," he said. He ran his fingers into her tousled hair, bringing her face against his chest.

She closed her eyes, then opened them. "I have to pick up Sophie at Lorrie's."

"In a minute." His voice was a deep purr, soothing, yet with that undercoating of rough excitement she found so alluring in this man.

"That was wonderful," she finally said.

"The best." He nuzzled his lips along her temple. "The very best, Carey Hall."

She caught the nuance. "That worries you."

He sighed. "Yeah, that worries me."

"Why?"

"You ask too many questions."

"It's the doctor in me. That's what we do." She licked

his chest and tasted salt. "Making love is work. I think it should be counted as an aerobic exercise."

That elicited a chuckle from him. "You have an amazing mind." He kissed her forehead, her cheek, her throat, then licked the moisture from between her breasts.

To her shock, she found she wanted to make love all over again. "I really have to go," she managed, fighting the selfish demands of her body.

"I know." He eased away from her and stood. He grabbed a tissue from the box on her desk and handed it to her.

"There's a bathroom through there."

They bathed and dressed, moving around each other with an ease she found as disturbing as the explosion of desire between them. There was puzzlement in his eyes, too.

At last, she stood by her desk, her cardigan on, her purse strap over her shoulder, her heavy coat in her hand. She checked the time.

It had been a little less than an hour ago that she'd gone to answer the door. She tried to decide if anything had really changed, but she didn't know.

"Well," she said.

"It's been fun," he finished for her, his smile slightly ironic, more than a little enigmatic. "The roads are slick. Be careful."

"I will. It's a short trip." She searched for her gloves. "I can't have lost them. I bought two pairs the other day."

He picked them off the floor behind her desk chair. "Are these what you're looking for?" He held them so she could put them on, then followed her out the side door.

His truck was parked behind her sports utility vehicle. He backed out, then let her get on the street before he fell in behind her. He followed her to Lorrie's, then to her house. Making sure she got home okay, she assumed.

As if she hadn't traveled these roads a million times. But it gave her a nice feeling that he did.

"Is that J.D.?" Sophie wanted to know. "Let's invite him in. Can he eat supper with us?"

Carey hesitated. "Okay." She pulled into the garage and climbed out, then waved her arm at the truck, indicating he should come into the garage with them. After a couple of seconds, the truck eased forward into the empty space. He rolled down the window.

"Would you like to have supper with us?" she asked. The question sounded ridiculously formal after what had just happened between them.

Wayne considered, for all of two seconds, then nodded. He turned the lights and the engine off. He needed to talk to Carey. He had to tell her who he was. Tonight. Before word got out all over town. He climbed down from the truck.

"Where's Freeway?" Sophie demanded, slipping her hand into his and skipping to keep up as they went into the house. "Didn't he come with you?"

"Not tonight. He was in the hay barn with his family, where it was warm and dry."

"He has a family?" Her eyes sparkled with interest. "What's his wife's name? Do they have any kids?"

"Yeah. Daisy is the, um, wife. They have four pups."

"Ohh, that sounds so nice."

The five-year-old studied her mom, who was busy turning on lights and removing her cardigan and gloves, which she stuck on a shelf next to the old-fashioned coatrack. He could almost see the wheels turning as Sophie tried to figure out how to wheedle a pup out of Carey.

Two cats greeted them in the kitchen. "That's Dudley and that's Pickles," Sophie introduced them.

The cats were old. They'd each lost a fang. Their muzzles were gray. One evidently had arthritis in its hips. Yeah, the kid could use a new pet.

"Help J.D. with his coat," Carey suggested.

"Okay." The kid pulled off her own winter wear and showed him where to hang his. "Would you like to watch the news on television? That's what Daddy likes to do."

Emotion tugged at his heart. "I'd rather stay here and watch your mom," he confessed.

Carey flashed him a worried glance, then went back to her chores. He pulled out a chair and straddled it. Sophie decided to color in a Donald Duck coloring book.

In a few minutes, wonderful odors wafted from a skillet in which Carey mixed wine and chicken breasts. She added dried onion that she'd soaked in hot water for a few minutes, then some other spices.

She placed potatoes in the microwave and started them to cooking. When they came out, frozen green beans went in. She scooped out the potatoes and added ranch dressing, then stuffed the mixture back into the potato skins. After laying strips of cheese on top, she stuck the potatoes in a toaster oven to brown.

"Sophie, you may set the table," she said.

"I'll help," he volunteered.

Within thirty minutes of entering the kitchen, he was sitting down to a mouthwatering meal that could have come from any fancy restaurant he'd ever been in. Chicken marsala, duchess potatoes, French-cut green beans with toasted almonds, a salad and white wine.

"You like to cook," he said when they were all seated around the oak table in the kitchen.

"Yes. I suppose it's my hobby."

They all held hands and the girls said grace together. Again he got a twangy feeling inside, as if a tightly wound guitar string had been plucked hard. There was danger here in this cozy kitchen.

"How are things at the ranch?" she asked. "Have you lost any cattle lately?"

He told her about the mineral block. She listened with a quiet, intent expression, her eyes troubled as he told of his suspicions. Sophie slipped bits of food under the table to the two cats. Carey pretended not to see.

They talked of local news. Carey included Sophie by asking about her day. With the enthusiasm of the young for detail, the kid told about a boy getting sick after lunch at school. Carey nodded solemnly and didn't reprimand her daughter for choosing a topic inappropriate to mealtime, as his own mother would have when he was young. His admiration for her as a mother and a person grew.

Therein lay the danger.

He was getting sucked in and way too comfortable with these two. He needed to back off. When the kid went to bed, he'd tell Carey who he was, then he'd leave. He needed some distance between them to get his bearings again.

After the meal, Carey put on coffee while Sophie went off to her room. When she returned, she was in blue fleecy pajamas with feet in them.

"I stuck my zipper," she said, stopping in front of him. She obviously expected him to fix it.

He took out his knife and cut a ball of fleece that was caught, removed it, then finished zipping the pajamas.

"Let's get your teeth brushed." Carey went to the back of the house with her daughter.

He decided to get off his duff and help with the dishes. While he rinsed and put them in the dishwasher, he listened to the wind and rain against the window. The coffeemaker gurgled pleasantly. It was a night for staying inside.

From down the hall, he heard water running and the sounds of the females as they chatted, laughter running through their conversation.

"Should I give J.D. a kiss good-night?" he heard Sophie ask. He found himself on edge waiting for the answer.

"If you'd like," Carey said after a brief hesitation.

They returned to the kitchen. "You want a hug and a kiss?" Sophie asked, fully expecting him to say yes.

"Sure."

She held her arms out. He lifted her up so she could reach him. She kissed his cheek and hugged him. He caught the scent of baby powder and toothpaste and little-girl smell. His insides did the strange, twangy thing again.

He kissed her cheek and hugged her back.

"You want to read me a story?"

"No, he doesn't," Carey cut in before he could reply. "He's done enough for you tonight."

The child wasn't daunted. "I've got a new book about a bear family," she told him. "They have two kids—a brother and a sister. I wish I had a brother or sister." Her gaze went to her mother in mute appeal. "I don't see why we can't have a baby. Lorrie's daughter did."

"Babies cry at night. A doctor has to sleep."

"Yeah. So she can take care of the sick people who come to see her," Sophie explained.

When he set her on her feet, she skipped happily down the hall, three steps in front of her mom.

He heaved a deep breath. Confession might be good for the soul, but it was damned hard on the nerves. He finished with the dishes, found a mug and helped himself to coffee.

The rain turned to sleet and clacked impatiently against the windows. A chill crept up his spine.

It was forty minutes before Carey returned. He'd changed his mind about telling her forty times.

"It's cold out there," she said, pouring a cup of coffee for herself. "We might have snow before morning."

"Yeah. Listen, there's something I need to tell you—"

"That's okay. I know tonight…earlier…didn't mean anything." She smiled briefly, a controlled, doctorish type of smile.

"The hell it didn't." He came up out of the chair, anger and other feelings driving him. He didn't like her blunt acceptance of casual sex between them.

He tipped her chin up and glared into her hazel eyes. She blinked once, startled, then glared right back. She looked so much like her daughter when the kid had put in her two cents about having a brother or sister that his anger dissolved, leaving all the other emotions, the ones he couldn't identify, swirling around in him.

"What is it?" she asked.

"You. Us. Everything." He kissed her then. He didn't mean to. He tried not to. But the need was stronger than common sense. He touched her mouth, and he was lost to reason and self-preservation.

Tell her, a voice warned inside him.

Later, another answered.

After a few seconds while she struggled not to respond, she parted her lips and gave him entry. He delved inside the warm honey of her mouth, while his body reared and plunged like a stallion sensing a mare in heat.

Her arms came around his shoulders. She arched against him, straining upward to meet the demands of his kiss just as she had earlier in her office.

"Where?" he muttered, biting and licking along her neck, knowing he wasn't going to quit until he'd sampled the entire feast that was her.

"At the end of the hall."

He lifted her off her feet.

"I'm heavy," she protested.

"Less than a bale of hay."

She sighed and snuggled her face into his neck. She kissed and nibbled and licked her way from his ear to his throat. He was rock hard and throbbing by the time he entered the bedroom. She flipped on a light switch. A lamp at either side of the bed came on.

"Wait." She closed and locked the door.

He set her on her feet beside the king-size bed and pressed her hands to her sides when she would have touched him. He removed her clothing piece by piece, stopping to shrug out of his own clothes, keeping them even, as he did.

She glanced at the light.

He turned off one, but left the other on, laying his shirt over the shade to soften the glow. That earned him a smile. She was just a tad shy, this woman who had dedicated herself to treating the human body.

As sure as the storm blew down from Crazy Mountain, he knew she hadn't had a man in this house since her husband had left it. She hadn't had another man period. Neither had he been interested in another woman since he'd met this one.

When they were both naked, he raked the covers back, braced one knee on the mattress and lowered them to the pristine expanse of white sheet.

A tremor raced through her slender form as he adjusted his body to the pleasing curves of hers.

"It's that way for me, too," he told her.

He lowered his head and kissed her breasts, running his tongue around the sensitive tips until they contracted into delicious little morsels that he tasted over and over.

Her cries were muted now, careful because of the child asleep down the hall, yet exciting and encouraging to his ears. Lying beside her, he glided his hand over her, watching the flush of sexual anticipation turn her skin from pale to rosy tones.

"Beautiful," he murmured.

He lingered at the feminine mound, smiling as he explored the springy blond curls there.

She touched the scars on his chest and along his arm. She traced a finger along the one on his thigh. She looked a question at him.

"'Nam," he said. "They rebuilt my kneecap after a land mine shattered it."

Sorrow mingled with the fires of desire inside her. She kissed the scars on his chest, tears in her eyes.

"It doesn't matter," he assured her. "Nothing does, not now. When you touch me, the past is gone. There's only this moment in time. And you and me."

It was the truth. Nothing from his past intruded on the enchantment between them.

He laid his hand on her breast, cupping the flesh that was both soft and firm under his palm. The nipple formed a tight, hard core in the middle of his hand. He rubbed around and around, reveling in the feel of this woman.

When she touched him intimately, he sucked in a harsh breath and sought control. Her incredibly smooth hands explored his body as he'd explored hers earlier, finding every sensitive inch of flesh. He forced himself to stay still and let her get used to him.

She stroked up and down, then cupped the area behind the hard shaft, tugging gently, experimentally, watching him all the while to gauge his reaction.

"That's very exciting," he said, drawing a slight smile from her. "It does to me what this does to you."

He caressed between her legs, his fingers finding the slick passage, then the sensitive nub that swelled with delight when he stroked her there. She was ready, but he wouldn't last a minute if he entered her. He roamed her body, his mouth hungry for the taste of her.

When he slipped his hands under her hips, she caught her breath in a gasp. He smiled into her eyes before lowering his head and finding that sexy little bit of flesh that responded so fully to his touch.

He took her to the peak, let her come down gently, then took her there again, using his fingers as well as his mouth to take her as high as she could go. She ran her fingers into his hair, then clutched him as she soared once more, her cries pressed into the pillow.

When she quieted, he slid over her slender length and entered her in one plunging, heated thrust, all the way to the hilt. He closed his eyes and held on for a moment before moving again.

Drawing on all his reserves of control, he watched her and began the journey to paradise all over again. She smiled up at him, so beautiful his breath locked in his throat.

She stroked up and down his thighs, then curved her hands around his hips, guiding him as he moved in her. Her eyes were half-closed. The smile lingered on her lips. She pulled him against her. Harder. Faster. Her hips rose to meet each thrust of his.

When she held her breath and closed her eyes tightly, he let go completely, burying himself in her, luxuriating in the intense throb of release, spending himself in her until he couldn't tell where her flesh ended and his began. They were one, and it was the most powerful sensation he'd ever experienced.

The climax went on and on until he was drained of energy. He rested on his arms for another moment, then shifted wearily to the side. He'd rest for a moment.

A moment, he reminded himself, unable to summon the energy to open his eyes. Then he'd tell her who he was.

Just one more moment of bliss, then he'd have to tell her...

One moment...

Seven

Carey awoke to the jangle of the alarm clock. She stretched, then groaned as muscles, well used the previous night, protested movement. The next thing she realized was her state of dress, or rather undress. She was stark naked. She jerked upright and stared at the other side of the bed.

J. D. Cade lay there.

He was watching her, his eyes wary even as a smile curved his mouth. "Waking up with someone is a shock after years of waking alone, isn't it?"

"'Shock' isn't the word for it," she stated, unable to believe she'd let a man spend the night with her…in her house…with her child right down the hall.

She was going to have to get up. She couldn't cower there all day with the covers clutched to her bosom like a frightened virgin. Which she definitely wasn't.

He made it easy for her by swinging out of bed. "Okay if I use your shower?" he asked, as if they'd done this every day for years.

"Yes," she croaked, unable to keep from staring at his lean strength while he crossed the carpet and entered the bathroom. She heard the shower come on.

"You can join me," he called.

There was a smile in his deep, rough voice, scarred from his ordeal in Vietnam. He carried other, less visible, scars after his experiences with life.

After another thirty seconds of indecision, she slipped from the bed and dashed into the bathroom. When she opened the shower door, his arms were there to welcome her.

He soaped her all over, his manner grave. She'd expected playful or at least sexual overtones. There was neither. His mood was introspective.

"Have you told the McCallums?" he asked.

"Not yet. I'm going to call them this morning." She leaned her head back and let the water rinse the shampoo out of her hair.

He soaped, then rinsed, then turned off the water.

The sudden quiet disturbed her. Without the noise of the shower around them, there was no sound to drown out the thoughts that clamored in her head.

She stepped out, grabbed a towel and tossed another to him. "Last night—"

"I shouldn't have stayed," he interrupted, finishing the sentence. "I meant to leave, but I fell asleep."

"I've never had…there's Sophie to think of…and other things," she finished lamely.

"Small-town gossip."

She nodded. "Lily Mae Wheeler lives on the next block down from here. If she sees the ranch truck—"

Lily Mae wasn't the only one who would notice. The baby-sitter lived three houses down the street. Annie drove by each day on her way to the hospital.

Carey sighed. She didn't want to think about it.

He finished drying off. "We'll sort it out." He went to one of the twin sinks.

"How?"

"However we need to."

It was hard to concentrate when he was flagrantly aroused. The towel wrapped around his waist couldn't disguise the fact. She turned away, heat flooding her face, when he caught her staring.

"Okay if I use your razor?" he asked.

She nodded and hurried into the bedroom where she applied deodorant and powder, then slipped into slacks and a turtleneck. She was putting on a brocaded vest that had reminded her of a Mississippi gambler when she'd seen it at the consignment shop, when he came into the bedroom.

He was dressed by the time she blow-dried her hair and combed it into place. He followed her to the kitchen.

"Eggs and bacon?"

"Just coffee will be fine."

She ignored the request and prepared a full breakfast. It was easier than thinking about them and what the future might hold. He sat at the table, seemingly deep in thought, while he watched her fix the meal.

"It's still raining," he remarked when she joined him.

"At least it isn't snow or ice."

It wasn't until they finished that he spoke what was in his mind. "I have something to tell you."

A chill attacked her heart. Her first thought was that he'd lied, that he was married and had a family somewhere.

"My name isn't J. D. Cade."

"What?" She stared at him blankly, his statement so far from what she'd imagined she couldn't respond to it.

"I made it up when I came back here."

She caught the nuance. "You've been here before?"

He nodded. "I used *J* because it was my father's initial and *D* because it was my brother's. Jeremiah and Dugin."

The facts sank slowly into her mind like a pebble tossed into a pond. The ripples spread in ever-widening circles, touching off other connections.

"And 'Cade' was short for Kincaid," she said, dazed by the information. "But there was no one left in the family—"

She stared at him as suspicion grew.

"I'm Wayne Kincaid. That's why I wanted to be tested as a donor. I'm Jennifer McCallum's brother."

She shook her head, trying to take it all in, to make sense of it. "Wayne died in Vietnam."

"No. I was captured, but I got away."

"You never came back."

"I couldn't. There was nothing left here. I wanted to

come back but there were too many obstacles. I hated my father. I wanted to escape the Kincaid name and all it stood for. It was easier to let everyone think I was dead."

"You'll have to tell now." She studied him, this stranger who had been in her arms last night. "Won't you?"

"Yes. Sam Brightwater has already guessed. I'm pretty sure Kate Walker has, too, after the hours we spent together during the cave-in. Her husband was my best friend once. I don't think Kate has told him any-thing though. I can't let Ethan find out from someone else. I was going to tell you last night."

"Only, I attacked you when you showed up at the office," she murmured in embarrassment.

"Hardly," he said with a trace of amusement in his tone. His face hardened. "Don't confuse what happened between us as a man and a woman with anything else."

She rubbed a hand across her forehead. "How can I not? Everything in a person's life impinges on every-thing else. In medicine, it's known as treating the whole patient." She sighed. "What a mess."

Staring at the toast crumbs on her plate, she realized people were like that—scattered across the landscape of life, made of the same elements, yet each separate, divided from all others by the randomness of life.

"Don't make a federal case of it," he cautioned.

"I don't know what to make of it. I don't know how I feel." She laughed without amusement. "But then, I didn't know how I felt before your great confession, either."

He came around the table. She stood, not sure whether to bolt or hold her ground. He clasped her upper arms.

"Yes, you do." His eyes gleamed with the flames of passion. "Nothing has changed between us."

He kissed her, causing her whirling thoughts to spin faster, throwing her world completely out of control. She clutched his waist as her legs trembled.

"Whatever was between us is still here," he said in satisfaction when he lifted his head. He tapped the middle of her chest, then his own.

"J.D.," she began, and stopped. "Wayne. The golden boy. The pride of the Kincaids. The best quarterback Whitehorn ever had." She drew a shaky breath. "It isn't the same."

"That boy died in 'Nam."

The bitterness in his tone penetrated her daze. She had seen his scars. She knew some of what he had endured. "But the memories will always be in you." She moved away from his embrace and stared out the window at the gloomy day. "Tell me," she requested. "Tell me all of it."

He helped himself to fresh coffee. "I went off to war when I was eighteen," he began. He talked of capture and pain, of escape and more pain, of more years in the service, of wandering the world, all in a few brief sentences that told her more than if he'd spoken for hours. He finished and fell silent, his gaze pensive.

"Do you need to speak to anyone else before I call Jessica and Sterling?" she asked.

"Not this minute, but don't tell them who I am."

The shortness of the answer reminded her of the role

he'd chosen for himself. Outsider. He wanted to stay that way, but that would be impossible.

"If you'd told us sooner, we could have saved a lot of time. We could have tested you when we tested Clint." Anger replaced the pity she'd felt listening to his story.

"I'd hoped he would match."

"So you wouldn't have to confess who you were…who you are. You'd have left without saying a word."

Bit by bit, it was dawning on her what a fool she'd been to trust this man. A loner. A drifter. She'd known that from the beginning. Now she also knew he'd been living a lie the whole time. She'd fallen for it just as she had with her ex-husband. Some people were slow to learn, it seemed.

"There was nothing to say. I don't want the ranch or any part of the Kincaid name. I was happy being free of it."

"Then why did you return?"

"I was near here on a construction job." He shrugged. "I was curious. I came over to see what had happened to the town. I found out I had a brother and sister and that the ranch was having problems. There seemed to be a mystery to solve, so I hired on when I found out Harding was having trouble keeping hands."

"The news of who you are will spread faster than gossip at a church social. You'll be hounded by reporters when it breaks," she warned him. "Your whole history will be endlessly relived and expounded upon. You died a hero. It's harder to return as simply a human."

"I'll survive." He resumed his seat. "When do you need me for the transplant?"

"Not for a while. We'll have to isolate Jenny and destroy all her bone marrow before we can proceed. I'll let you know." She shifted gratefully into her medical role. "Stay out of crowds and away from anyone with a cold. I don't want you coming down with anything."

He nodded. "I'll stick to the ranch. It's pretty much isolated now that everyone thinks it has a curse. Only Lester Buell sniffs around, wanting to buy it for a song in his usual scruffy manner."

Carey studied the scowl on his face. She tried to bring up the picture of the boy who had tripped over her, then had bought her another ice-cream cone, with the man who stood before her. She couldn't.

He was right. That boy had left a long time ago and never returned. This hardened, embittered man had taken the golden boy's place.

Although she'd never really known him, she mourned that boy and his shattered ideals, his beautiful body and its youthful perfection. Out of the twin fires of tragedy and pain this man had been born.

She went to the wall telephone and dialed the Mc-Callums' number. Sterling answered.

"I have news," she said. She hesitated to call it good news. The transplant might not take. "We have a donor."

There was the expected moment of stunned silence.

"Thank God," Sterling said. "Who?"

"It's…J. D. Cade." She glanced across the room. "I think he wants to come by and talk to you."

Wayne nodded agreement when she looked his way. There was distrust coupled with pity and anger in her eyes. He had a lot of confessing to do today, a lot of fences to mend. Carey might be one he couldn't repair.

At any rate, he needed to reassure the deputy of his intentions toward the ranch. Then he had to talk to Kate and Ethan. And Clint Calloway. And Reed Austin. Then the sheriff and the ranch foreman. The list was growing longer…

"Okay, I'll tell him." She finished and hung up. "He wants you to come by before he goes to the office at eight."

His eyes went to the clock on the stove. "Seven-thirty. I suppose I'd better run."

She nodded, her gaze averted from his. She was raising barriers and No Trespassing signs like quills coming up on a porcupine. He could hardly blame her. He'd lived a lie and let her and the town believe that lie. Now he'd have to pay the consequences.

He put on his coat and headed for the door. "I guess I'm through running," he said, and went out into the cold.

The lights were on in the ranch house when Wayne pulled up at the Walker place. He cut the engine and sat there in the pickup, reluctant to face the family. Inside, he saw a woman's head outlined in the window.

Probably Kate trying to determine who was out there.

He climbed down and went to see them—the woman he'd once loved more than anyone and the man who'd been his best friend through most of his school years.

He owed it to them to tell the truth before someone passed the news on to them. He'd told the McCallums that morning and Clint Calloway that afternoon. Time had definitely run out for him.

Kate had the door open when he stopped in front of it. "J.D.," she said, her eyes puzzled. "This is a surprise."

He nodded. "Hello, Kate. Ethan."

Ethan held a hand out without getting up. A kid lay in his lap, sound asleep. Wayne shook hands and took the chair Kate indicated.

"It's cold out tonight. Would you like a cup of hot cider to warm you?" she offered. "We were just going to have some ourselves."

"That would be fine." His smile felt tight. Hell, his skin felt tight over his whole body. He should have told Kate the truth when they were trapped—

"What brings you out this way?" Ethan asked with more than a tad of suspicion.

Wayne couldn't blame him for that. He suspected Ethan was a little jealous of Kate. "I needed to talk to you." He studied her when she returned to the room with two cups and a platter of cookies.

She was a beautiful woman. He was proud of how she'd turned out. A judge, by damn. That was something. And married to Ethan. Catching the light in his old friend's eyes when she handed him the cup, Wayne knew the marriage was good for both Ethan and Kate.

He relaxed.

"I'm going to put the baby to bed and check on Darcy," Kate murmured. "If you fellows will excuse me?"

"Sure," Ethan said.

Wayne noted the confidence in Ethan's touch as he lifted the sleeping baby to Kate's shoulder. It brought a lump to his throat. Everyone seemed to have families to come home to, except him.

"Something about the ranch?" Ethan asked, jogging him back to the topic at hand.

"No. It's about you and me and Kate, about who we are. And about who we were once upon a time when we were all young and we were friends."

Ethan stiffened. He leaned forward, his eyes narrowing as he stared into Wayne's eyes. Wayne met his gaze levelly.

"My God," Ethan said. "What are you saying?"

"I think you've figured it out."

"Kate, you'd better come in here," Ethan called.

"Just a sec."

The minutes ticked by as the two sat in stunned silence. He saw Ethan's hand tremble as he lifted his cup to his mouth. Kate returned to the living room, a concerned smile on her face.

"What is it?" she asked, alarm crossing her expression when she saw her husband staring at their guest.

"Tell her who you are," Ethan ordered in a hoarse voice laced with growing anger.

Kate sat beside Ethan and took his hand before turning to study Wayne. She frowned and looked from one man to the other. "What's going on?"

"Katie, my girl, you'll grow into a fine woman one of these days," Wayne said softly, the way he had years ago when he'd teased her.

She shook her head slightly as if to clear it. "There was someone who used to say that to me—" She clasped both hands over her mouth, then to her breast. "Wayne. Oh, my God. Wayne. I thought…when we were in the cave-in, but I couldn't be sure…. No. It can't be."

Ethan put an arm around her and held her close.

Wayne thought of the hours he and Kate had spent trapped in an old mining shaft months ago. While waiting to be rescued, he'd thought of a thousand things to say to her. He hadn't said any of them. Looking into her eyes, he knew she had suspected who he was at that time, but her rational mind couldn't accept it then.

"It is, Katie," Wayne confessed. "I've wanted to tell you, both of you, for a long time, but…" He shook his head, helpless to explain how he'd felt.

"But what?" she demanded. "But it was easier to let us think you were gone? To let us mourn for you all these years? My God, the grief we've been through. And the guilt. How could you leave us here wondering—"

"Hush, Kate," Ethan murmured, pulling her against him protectively. "I want to hit him myself, but maybe there's an explanation." He glanced at Wayne. "There damn well better be an explanation."

Wayne nodded.

"How did you live? I saw that grenade explode under you. I saw you blown to bits."

"The kid took most of it. I got a load of shrapnel in the chest and neck, some in the legs, bloody, but nothing major hit, not my lungs or heart. Not even my face."

"What happened to you after that? The platoon pulled out. You were left for dead." Ethan kept staring at him as if he expected someone to declare this was all a joke, one in very bad taste.

"I was captured. I spent the next six months in a bamboo cage."

Kate gasped. "How did you get away?" Her face was the color of wallpaper paste.

"The soldier in the cage with me nearly drove me crazy moaning day and night with his wounds. He was gut shot. I was lucky. I healed. My jaw was broken, though. It set crooked. Later, the surgeons rebroke it and set it again."

Ethan rubbed his jaw as if experiencing the pain of having it broken twice.

Wayne took a breath and continued. "Anyway, I got an idea. I started moaning, too, but only at night, then I started screaming. I kept it up no matter what they did. Finally they moved the cage out to the end of the rice field. I got louder. They moved us into the jungle. I screamed all night. As soon as it was nearly light, I kicked out the side and took off."

Kate pressed a hand over her mouth.

"The other guy was pretty bad. I carried him for a while. Then he started fighting me, thinking I was the enemy. He broke away, ran a few feet and stepped on a land mine. The blast finished him and did some damage to my legs, but I was lucky. I ran into an American platoon five days later. I guess I was pretty much of a mess. The medics fixed me up and had me evacuated. I spent a year in the hospital in Hawaii. They reset my jaw and patched my arm, then they rebuilt my kneecap—"

"Oh, Wayne," Kate murmured. She reached across the coffee table and squeezed his arm.

He swallowed hard as a knot balled in his throat. "I'd been gone for over four years by then. I wasn't able to write to you for two years. I figured you both would have forgotten me by then."

"Never," she said.

Ethan nodded agreement.

"It was my memories of you, Katie, of both of you…" He looked at Ethan, including him. "Of the three of us, of the good times we shared, of laughter and being young, that kept me going until I got back to American lines. I made a splint for my leg, then walked, sometimes crawled, heading south, always south, and thought about you two. That's all I thought about…of being home…with you…the way we used to be."

Ethan covered his face with a hand. Tears pooled, then fell from Kate's eyes as she stared at him with horror and pity warring in her expression.

He stood, as emotions too strong to be denied washed over him. He had to get away….

Ethan and Kate rose, too. Then somehow they were in one another's arms, and he knew it was all right. They were going to forgive him. He loved them. God, he loved them, these friends…ah, God….

They talked most of the night, catching up on one another's lives, sharing the loneliness and the guilt.

"I'm glad you two found each other." He gave them

a stern frown. "Even if it was damn late. You've made a good home for those kids." He punched Ethan in the ribs. "You a daddy. Never thought I'd see the day."

His friend grinned in that reserved way he'd always had. "The woman just wouldn't leave me alone. It got embarrassing—"

His breath huffed out as Kate gave him a none-too-gentle nudge with her elbow.

"It's four o'clock," she said in surprise. "How about some breakfast? I don't think any of us will sleep now." She led the way into the kitchen. "You nearly told me who you were when we were trapped in that cave-in, didn't you?"

Wayne nodded. "I wanted to. Hell, I wanted to make love to you." He glanced at Ethan. "But I could see you were head over heels in love with this guy. Can't figure out why, though. He looks like a rough piece of rawhide left outdoors for the winter."

The two men fell to sparring, then ended up pounding each other on the shoulder while Kate got out sausage and eggs. They ate and talked some more as the sun came up.

At last Wayne pulled on his hat and coat. "I've got things to do today. I'm the donor for the bone marrow transplant for Jenny McCallum. We matched up."

"Damn!" Ethan exclaimed. "She's your half sister. And Clint Calloway is your half brother."

"Right." He shook his head. "It seems odd to have family I never knew. Everything has changed so much."

Kate touched his arm gently. "Carey Hall is a good woman," she said softly.

He met her knowing gaze and felt a flush creep up his neck into his face. "Yeah, she is that."

"You could stay here, build a new life. The ranch needs you—"

"No, Katie. That life is over. I'm not going to claim any part of it."

"But you came back," Ethan stated.

"Maybe it was a mistake."

"No," Kate disagreed firmly. "Don't keep on running away. You belong here."

Long after he drove off toward the ranch, her words echoed in his mind. He shook his head. He hadn't belonged anywhere in twenty-five years.

Freeway greeted him with a joyous yelp when he parked and climbed out of the truck. He rubbed the mutt's ears. A tugging at his pant leg drew his attention.

One of the pups had a hold on the denim and was waging a fierce battle with it. Another had a similar hold on Freeway's tail. Freeway gave him a patient glance that seemed to say, Kids. What can you do with them these days?

Wayne chuckled past the lump that insisted on forming in his throat again. "Right, old man. A family takes a lot of care." He set the pup aside and headed for his bunk and a few hours of sleep before he talked to the sheriff, then the others on the list.

The news went through the town as fast as telephones and the grapevine could carry it. Curse or no curse, a herd of reporters laid siege to the ranch during the next week, demanding interviews. Wayne told his life story so many times he began to think of recording it and just handing out a tape cassette when anyone came around.

He came down with a cold within three days. Carey called him two days after that.

"Can you stop by for blood work in the morning?" she asked, sounding very professional.

"I have a cold."

"Oh. When did you come down with it?"

He told her.

"Okay, we'll schedule you for next week. Drop by my office, say, at six on Monday. That'll be after-hours so you won't run into anyone with an infection."

"Sure."

After he hung up, he realized his heart was pounding. He missed her. One night with her, and he missed her.

Walking out of the ranch office, he tripped over one of the puppies that had gotten out of the barn. He picked it up and scratched its ears. The pup licked his face, in ecstasy at being petted.

"It's time for you to leave home. There's a kid you'll fall in love with who needs a dog."

The puppy yapped excitedly as if he knew exactly what had been said. Wayne smiled. Maybe this would help store up some good points with Carey.

Carey straightened medical books that didn't need it and rearranged her desktop, which was already neat. She'd watered her plants. She flopped in the chair and found herself staring at the sofa. Images whirled in her head of heat and passion and entwined bodies. She groaned and pressed her face into her hands. Why, why, why had she behaved so foolishly? Worse, why did she want to do it all again?

A knock sounded at the side door. Every muscle in her body jumped. Her heart went into racing mode.

"Coming," she called, and dashed down the hall. She unlocked the door and opened it.

J.D.—no, Wayne Kincaid—stood on the step. He seemed to loom over her, tall and lean, as wary as a stray dog, and so damn desirable she nearly threw herself at him.

Again.

"Come on in," she said in her best professional voice. "I have some papers for you to fill out first."

She fled back to the office, while her heart fluttered and did diving tricks and generally misbehaved.

He followed behind her, his expression unreadable.

"Here, these are release forms. You won't be able to sit a horse for a few days after the procedure. It will make your hip somewhat sore."

"Sore as hell," he muttered.

She glanced at him, wondering if he was thinking of changing his mind.

"'Somewhat sore' is doctor talk for 'sore as hell,'" he clarified. "I learned that during my previous stay in the army hospital." He grinned, looking surprisingly like a kid who was proud of figuring out some adult secret.

"Yes, sore as hell," she echoed. "Since your right leg

is the damaged one, I thought we'd take the marrow from your left hip."

"So I can limp on both sides?" He glanced over the release, then signed it and handed it to her.

She looked at the name he'd used. Wayne Kincaid. "I hadn't noticed any limp."

"It's only when I get tired. My right knee stiffens up sometimes."

After nodding in understanding, she gestured toward the hall. "I'd like to get your medical history now and do the preliminary checkup."

"Anything you say, Doc." He was mockingly agreeable.

She weighed him, checked his height, took his blood pressure and did all the things her nurse usually did. She had him fill out the standard medical history.

Her eyes misted when she read of the year spent in Hawaii, most of it in the hospital. Six operations for surgical repair. She imagined bones broken and flesh mangled by a grenade and a land mine. The waste of it.

"There's that heavy sigh," he said. "How's the kid doing? I heard you've put her in the hospital, that she's in some kind of strange contraption and you won't even let her mother in to see her."

"Jennifer's in a special isolation unit. It's rather like a big plastic bubble, but she can see and talk to people. We've set up a television, and Jenny has a remote control in the bubble. Sophie comes to the hospital and plays with her nearly every day. They play with games and interactive stories on the TV, each of them from her side of the plastic wall."

She realized she was rambling and stopped.

"So when do I report in?"

"In the next couple of days if possible. You're running a slight fever. I'd like to put you in isolation, too, and administer a round of antibiotics, then run the blood tests again before we proceed."

"All right. Two days from now. Where and what time?"

"Nine o'clock at the hospital." She closed and locked his file in the cabinet. Grabbing her purse and cardigan, she looked around for her gloves.

"Here." He lifted them off a shelf of medical books.

She stuffed them in her sweater pocket and walked with him down the hall, shutting off lights as they left.

Driving down the dark street, her breath as visible as a fog each time she exhaled, she longed for springtime and warmth and leisurely walks. Not that she ever had much time for leisure, but it was something to dream about.

Behind, Wayne followed in his truck, staying a careful distance behind her. She was *not* going to invite him in.

He didn't wait to be asked, but remained with her while she beeped the horn and Sophie ran out and joined her, then pulled into her drive behind her.

"Hi," Sophie yelled, jumping out. "Did Freeway—"

She got no further before the dog leaped out of the truck and ran straight for the girl. They hugged and kissed and laughed and barked.

"Nothing like being in love," Wayne said. He hefted

a box from inside the truck. "Freeway brought you a birthday present," he said to the child.

Carey eyed the box suspiciously.

"What?" Sophie ran to Wayne. "It isn't my birthday."

"It isn't?" Wayne acted surprised. "Well, he thought it might be close."

"It is. It's—" She looked at her mom.

"Only about five months away," Carey supplied.

"Yeah, that's close enough. Let's go inside."

Carey found herself trailing the cowboy, her daughter and the dog into the kitchen. He set the box on the floor and stood back.

Sophie pulled it open. "Ohh," she cried. "Oh, he's beautiful." She lifted out a puppy that wriggled with joy at the attention. Sophie hugged it to her, while Freeway licked her face. "What kind is it?" she asked.

"Part sheepdog and part mutt," he told her.

"Just like his father," Carey muttered. "You could have asked first."

Wayne gave her an amused glance, his eyes daring her to do something about the gift. As if she could with Sophie holding on to the pup for dear life.

"A kid needs a young pet," he said. "Not two old stodgy cats you probably got when you were her age."

"Hardly."

They'd been strays she'd adopted in high school. She realized that had been a long time ago.

She tossed her purse on a chair, hung up her sweater and stuck her gloves in a drawer. Two other pairs were there—a fact that annoyed her. She'd looked all over the house for the blasted things last week.

After washing her hands, she began supper. Wayne— she still thought of him as J.D.—and Sophie and the two dogs played tug-of-war over in the corner, out of her way.

She prepared Swedish meatballs and served them over spinach noodles, along with steamed broccoli and fresh carrot curls. She was aware when their guest left the girl and dogs and leaned against the counter, his incredibly blue eyes on her, his hands tucked into his pockets.

Her blood went hot just thinking of his touch. He'd caressed her all over, had made the most wonderful love to her, and it had all been a lie.

"I had better be going. I brought some puppy chow over. Shall I bring it in?"

She frowned at him. "Sophie would run away from home if I tried to pry her away from the pup. As you well know. Yes, bring it in."

He grinned at her tone and sauntered out, then returned in a swirl of cold air with the bag of dog food. "Freeway, it's time we were heading out."

Freeway thumped his tail and stayed put.

"I have dinner nearly ready," Carey said irritably. "You may as well stay."

"Since you put it so graciously, how can we refuse?"

She wanted to hit him with the stirring spoon. She set the table, told the other two to wash up and scolded herself for inviting him to dinner. It was just asking for trouble.

He and Sophie kept up a steady stream of chatter during the meal. He offered lots of advice on training the pup, then asked her what she was going to call it.

This took several minutes of serious thought. "I

was going to name him Buzz, but I don't know. That would leave Woody out." She looked at Freeway. "I know. Highway."

"Oh, honey, I don't think—" Carey broke off when Wayne chuckled, then tried to hide it behind a cough. "Highway?" she started again. "It's a bit unusual."

"I like it," Sophie declared.

Her chin set in that stubborn way that reminded Carey of the girl's father. Carey knew when to give in gracefully. "Highway it is."

"Good choice," he said.

She glared at him. But soon his arrogant grin and the absurdity of the name softened her mouth.

"Watch it. You're about to smile. Look, Sophie, your mom is smiling. She likes the name."

Sophie grinned happily, her gaze on her new friend. Carey felt misgivings tug at her heart. Her daughter was half in love with the elusive cowboy. Sophie gave her trust so readily, just as she once had.

After ice cream and homemade cookies, she was ordered to sit at the table while the other two cleared the dishes and cleaned the kitchen. Her worries increased as Sophie was drawn more and more to their guest.

She watched them put the box in the utility room and settle the puppy there to sleep with an old sock belonging to Sophie. Wayne laid out newspapers on the floor in case of accidents while the pup learned the ropes.

As soon as it was polite, she took her child from his presence and supervised the bath ritual, firmly rejecting the idea that Highway needed a bath, too. She took an extra long time with the bedtime story and a brief chat about the day's happenings. When she turned off the light, closed the door and returned to the kitchen, she found him still there.

"Thank you for the dog. Sophie adores it. You were right about her needing a young pet." She waited for him to leave, standing close to the door so she could show him out.

He rose, but didn't retrieve his coat. Instead, he came to her. "Relax, Doc," he told her. "This isn't going to hurt a bit."

She summoned the words to protest. They never got past her lips. He covered her mouth with his, taking the kiss deep and stirring her blood with memories of their other kisses. Those seemed almost a dream now.

"Invite me to stay." He nuzzled down her neck.

"No."

"For an hour."

"No."

"You might need help with the pup." There was laughter in his tone.

"No."

"Don't you know any other word?"

"No."

He sighed and lifted his head. "Stubborn."

She agreed. "But there's no need in continuing something that has no place to go."

He was silent for a long minute. "You're right. As soon as things are cleared up here, I'll be heading out."

Which was exactly what she'd thought he would do.

Long after he and Freeway were gone, she sat in front of the fire, not thinking, not feeling. At last she sighed and went to bed. She'd been in danger of falling in love, but she was okay now. She was over it.

Eight

Carey signed the admitting form, then looked it over. She handed it to the waiting clerk and hurried off to the nursing station in pediatrics. She wasn't going to stand around waiting for Wayne to show up. She had work to do.

At nine, she went to her office and began the next part of her day with the usual cases of flu and colds.

At eleven, she removed a dried bean from a four-year-old's nose and blobs of mashed potato from the ears of a two-year-old, which had affected his hearing. His mother was furious with his elder brother when she found out what the problem had been.

At noon, Carey dashed back to the hospital. She was supposed to meet Kane Hunter, who would do the actual bone marrow removal from Wayne, for a consultation.

"Has Kincaid checked in?" she asked, pausing by the admissions desk.

"Yes. Room 222."

"Thanks." She hurried to the elevator. She wanted to check on Jennifer first.

The anesthesiologist was talking to the child. Kane, dressed in surgical greens, stood beside the other doctor, his face grave. Jessica waited nearby, looking more than a little haggard after days of hospital living. She went home only when Sterling was there to spell her with their daughter.

A pain rippled through Carey's heart as she surveyed Jenny's listless form, lying on the bed in her bubble. The usually cheerful little girl had cried last night, not wanting to take another shot. Jessica had wept, too.

Carey had sent the mother to the ladies' room to freshen up, then she'd talked to Jennifer about getting through this last stretch and being strong for her mommy and daddy.

"When you're all well and playing with your friends again, you'll be glad," she'd said to reassure the child.

Or else the little girl would be…gone.

Carefully, as if she herself might come apart, she inhaled, fighting the tears that threatened. Finally, the technique worked and she went forward.

"Well, look what the cat dragged up," Kane remarked, drawing a brief smile from Jenny when she saw Carey. "Is your other patient ready?" he asked.

"I haven't been to his room yet. I wanted to check on Jenny first. How are you feeling, sport?"

"Okay." Jenny looked at her with those incredibly blue Kincaid eyes. "I want the bone stuff."

"How about tomorrow morning, first thing?" Carey glanced at the two doctors. They both nodded.

"Then I can go home?" Jenny demanded, her spirits stirring at the thought.

"If the bone marrow takes. We'll have to give it a few days to get used to your body and to find a new home in your bones." Carey smiled with all the confidence she could muster. If determination counted, she knew they would win.

"Show me again," Jenny demanded.

Carey showed her the chart of the human body and traced the point where Wayne's bone marrow cells would be inserted in her bloodstream.

"Does it have to be another shot?" Jenny asked, her face puckering in distress. She looked at Jessica.

"This one is the most important," Jessica said with a brave smile. "As soon as it takes, we'll plan a party to thank your doctors. Ice cream and cake for everyone."

"I'll come as a clown," Kane volunteered.

That drew another faint smile.

"I'd better see about Wayne," Carey mentioned.

Kane fell into step beside her. "I'll go with you."

They reached room 222 and went in. Wayne was in bed, looking a bit peeved. "Do I have to lie around in a hospital gown until tomorrow?" he demanded.

"Yes," she said unequivocally.

Kane hid a smile. "I've looked at your X rays," he said to the grumpy patient. "You have a bone spur on your hip. I can remove that when I get the marrow. That should take care of that twinge you get when the spur hits the nerve that runs down to your leg."

Wayne eyed both of them suspiciously. "I don't have insurance."

"No charge. It'll be part of the service." Kane smiled and waggled his eyebrows like a mad scientist about to dissect an interesting subject.

Carey had been shocked when she'd examined the X rays. Although he'd told her of his injuries, she found he'd glossed over the truth. She hadn't been prepared for the bone breaks and scar tissue she and Kane had found. There was a metal rod in one leg where bone had been taken out completely, too shattered to mend normally. The kneecap was synthetic, too. She couldn't believe he hadn't lost the leg.

"Huh," Wayne said, a grin lifting the corners of his mouth. He and Kane were similar in their sense of humor. "Are you going to be there?" he asked her.

She nodded.

Kane ruffled her curls. "She's worse than a mother hen. She questions every decision made about any of her patients. Drives the hospital staff right up the wall."

"She's a bossy woman," Wayne agreed.

He tossed her an oblique glance that had her blood pressure shooting up, she realized.

"I'll see you in the morning at seven sharp," Kane told the patient. He explained briefly what he planned to do, then left after shaking hands with Wayne.

Carey stayed behind, looking over his chart as if figuring out clues in a treasure hunt.

"Well, Doc, will I live?" he finally quipped.

She tucked the chart under her arm. "Yes. With the additional procedure, you'll need to take it easy for several days. No riding, either horses or in the truck on rough roads."

He shrugged, totally unconcerned. "No problem."

"Who will look after you?"

"Freeway and I been taking care of each other for a long time." His grin was a challenge.

"I'm serious. Who's at the ranch?"

"Harding and four cowboys."

"No women?"

"Nah. The foreman's wife is staying with her brother. She's expecting, and Rand thinks the ranch is too dangerous for a woman at the present."

"Who does the cooking? Who cleans all those rooms?"

"The big house is closed," he informed her. "We hang out in the bunkhouse. This may come as a shock, but men know how to cook. We can also handle a washing machine."

His slow smile did things to her heart. She ignored it. "Yes, but you won't feel like getting up and down much tomorrow afternoon. I suppose I can keep you an extra day."

"Nix on that. I'll be fine. One of the boys can fix me a plate when they come in for supper."

"You'll need someone to drive you home."

"Oh. Well, Harding can do that."

"Where's your truck?"

"In the parking lot. Why?" He eyed her warily.

"Someone will need to drive it for you."

"My right leg is okay."

She studied his expression, which was closed and defensive. He wouldn't ask anyone for help if his life depended on it. Stubborn as a mule. She frowned at the realization and wondered what to do.

"Why did I have to come in so early?" he demanded.

"So we can make sure you don't have anything you might give Jenny that would kill her."

At her blunt answer, he subsided. She watched him flip on the television and channel-surf until he found a news program. She tried not to remember the last time she'd seen him in bed. In her bed, to be precise. It was impossible.

The magic of the passion they'd shared swept over her, making her blood sparkle as if she'd received a transfusion of the finest champagne. Forcing herself to act like the professional she was supposed to be, she explained the entire procedure to him, including the fact that the lab would be up for more blood for the final tests.

"The vampires have already been in." He held his arm out to show her the bandage. "They only took a couple of pints this time." His grin invited her to laugh.

She couldn't. She looked at the sheet covering his long legs and thought of being entangled with him beneath the covers. Heat built inside her. "I've got to go," she said, turning from the intriguing and much too tempting sight.

"Running?" he asked softly.

"Yes." Then she fled.

* * *

"Got it," Kane murmured, and hit the button.

The laser beam dissolved the bone spur that pressed a nerve bundle coming out of the spinal cord. Wayne would walk and move more easily in the future, without the twinge Kane had mentioned yesterday.

More than a twinge, Carey acknowledged. He must have been in pain often the past couple of years. She was glad they could do this for him.

Kane finished the procedure quickly and closed the puncture wound efficiently. Wayne would have nothing to show for his pain but a square of gauze and a strip of tape.

Carey breathed a sigh of relief and followed Kane out of surgery.

"Did you tell him he can't move around too much for a few days while he heals?" he asked.

"Yes."

The senior doctor chuckled. "Did he listen?"

"Is he male?" They exchanged grins.

"He needs to let his body reabsorb the spur completely before he strains the joint again. He could get severe arthritis if he doesn't."

"I'll tell him," she promised. A plan formed in her mind. Not that he would listen, but he was a sort of captive audience, so to speak.

She considered the crazy idea again. She was going to do it. She tossed the surgical smock into the bin along with the mask and head cover and booties. Soon they would inject Jennifer McCallum with her half brother's bone marrow. Then they would wait and see....

Wayne awoke to a gentle prodding. The scent of antiseptic tickled his nostrils, then a lighter, more pleasant aroma, one more familiar to him, teased him into opening his eyes. Carey bent over him.

"Here," she said. "Orange juice. That will take the dry taste out of your mouth."

"Thanks," he mumbled around a hospital straw. He drank, then pushed himself upright. Pain tore through him. A groan forced its way out of his throat.

"Easy."

"This is like 'Nam all over again," he groused, slumping back against the pillow.

"I know. It'll be worse tomorrow."

"If you speak another word in that bright-as-a-spring-robin tone, I'll have to choke you."

She dared to laugh outright. He wanted to pull her down on top of him and inhale her female sweetness until the pain was suffocated by passion. However, he didn't think that was going to happen today. For one thing, she wouldn't let him. For another, he felt like hell.

Just as she'd warned him.

"What happens next?" he asked.

She lifted her brows in question.

"To Jennifer. Have you given her the transplant?"

"Hours ago. You've slept all morning."

His glance went to the window. Late-afternoon light

cast long, slanted shadows against the glass. "I need to get back to the ranch. Work to be done."

Her hands flattened against his chest as if he had actually tried to get up. He liked the feel of them on him.

"Not today. At least, not by you," she amended. "You can't sit a horse for a few days or ride in the truck on those rough cow trails you call roads over on the Kincaid place. I'm having a grader work on my place."

"Costs money," he warned.

Damn, if he couldn't get around, how the hell were they going to catch Dale Carson and find out who he was working for? It would be up to the cop to get the info out of the sister. Not that Austin would find that a hardship.

"What's so funny?" she asked.

He studied Carey. She looked a little tattered around the edges. It had been a hard day. She'd come in before he went to surgery that morning and evidently stayed with him until it was over. That fact made him feel… funny.

Yeah, right. The situation was a barrel of laughs.

"Doctors," he responded to her question. "Hunter said I would be sore as hell when I woke up. Sore as hell means you feel as if you've been run over by a truck."

"Hey, you're a fast learner."

She laughed when he scowled. He wanted to hear it again—that sweet, feminine gurgle. He wanted to hear it while he made love to her. He groaned once more as desire tightened muscles he didn't want to move at the present.

"Tomorrow," he whispered. "We'll make love tomorrow."

Her hazel eyes opened wide, then crinkled at the corners as she laughed again. "You are incorrigible."

"Yeah, I knew there was a word for it." He managed a grin. "When do I get to see Jennifer?"

She went solemn. "Whenever you wish."

"Now?"

"Okay. It's time for you to leave. We'll stop by on the way out."

He studied the cold, gray sky outside the window. "You're going to throw me out in the snow?"

"The storm isn't due in until tonight. We'll have you safe and snug inside before then."

It sounded like a promise he couldn't refuse.

To his disappointment, an older nurse with gray hair that reminded him of a helmet came in to help him dress. Carey disappeared. The nurse brought a wheelchair with her. He managed not to groan while he pulled his clothes on.

"I can walk," he told Attila the Hun.

"Sit," she said.

He eyed her two hundred solid-packed pounds and decided to let her wheel him out of the hospital. She'd probably throw him into the truck. Then he'd head for the ranch.

Carey was with Jenny and Jessica when he arrived in style. She cast him a sly grin while Attila set the brake on the chair.

"Jennifer, look who's here," Jessica said. "This is Wayne, your other half brother."

"Like Clint?" the girl asked, watching him with the unwavering stare of a child.

"Like Clint," Carey confirmed. "Wayne was the one who gave you some of his bone marrow. Neat, huh?"

"Yes." Jenny smiled at him.

He saw a trace of the child he'd first met and fallen in love with months ago. Again he felt that strange twang in the vicinity of his heart.

"I don't know," he drawled, and rubbed his chin. "Next thing she might be chewing tobaccy and spittin' on the sidewalk and using swearwords just like I do."

Jenny's eyes rounded in surprise at his jest. She laughed. It sounded more like a weak frog on its last croak. He got that twang again.

"You don't do that," Jenny protested, covering her laugh with hands as frail as eggshells.

"Well, you never can tell when I might start. You just be real careful if you get a yen to chew."

"Or tell me," Carey invited. "I'm sure I have medicine to cure the urge." She gave him a narrow-eyed gaze. "In fact, maybe I'd better start you on it tonight. It tastes really terrible and is guaranteed to get rid of bad habits." She cackled in glee, drawing another laugh from the child, before glancing at her watch.

"We've got to go," she announced.

She sashayed out, leaving Wayne with the guardian nurse, who wheeled him down to admissions and had him sign some more papers before wheeling him to the emergency entrance.

His thoughts strayed stubbornly to Carey as he rolled along. He'd seen a new side to her here in the hospital. That she cared for her patients was obvious. There was a tenderness in her that grabbed a man by the throat. Her sense of humor worked well with her young charges, too. A man would be lucky to have a woman like her....

Carey was waiting in his truck when they arrived at the emergency room doors. "Hop in," she called.

"What the heck?" he said, not sure what was going on.

"Hurry. Sophie and Highway are waiting. They have a surprise supper for you."

His heart nearly beat itself out of his chest as he half climbed, half floated—with a little help from Attila—into the truck. The door slammed.

They were on their way. He didn't ask where they were going. Or how long he'd be staying.

Carey drove into the garage at her house and hit the button to close the door. Wayne hadn't said a word on the short trip to her house. She worried that she was being presumptuous in bringing him here. Now that the deed was done, she had more than a few misgivings about her decision which had seemed so logical yesterday.

"I thought you might want to stay here for a day or two," she said. "Lorrie will be here each morning. She or I will prepare lunch. Or I can take you out to the ranch, if you prefer." It had seemed important that he have someone to look after him for the first few days, but now she felt foolish for having assumed he'd want to stay with her.

He smiled, a white flash in the gloom of the garage. "I think I could endure your company for a few days."

His voice stroked over her the way his hands had, rough yet gentle. A crackle of electricity swept over her nerves. "Good." She'd spoken more briskly than she'd intended.

He shot her a glance, then opened the door and swung down. She dashed around the truck to help him.

"What about your ute?" he asked.

"Annie is going to give me a lift in the morning. I'll get it then." She got a cane out of the back of the truck. "Here, use this."

She hovered around him while he hobbled into the house. A sheen of perspiration covered his face by the time he made it up the steps and into the kitchen.

Lorrie, Sophie and Highway were there to greet them. The kitchen smelled of baking bread and ravioli. For a few minutes, there was confusion as the puppy barked and jumped around their feet. Sophie wanted to share some tale from school and Carey introduced the housekeeper to Wayne.

"I went to school with you," Lorrie exclaimed. "I was Lorenza Pike in those days. And twenty pounds lighter."

"You look just as gorgeous as I remember," Wayne said gallantly, scenes of long ago days filling his mind.

Carey ushered him to a chair and propped the cane against the wall when he was seated. She hung their coats up, then went to change clothes. In her bedroom, she hesitated to put on her old shapeless sweats, then frowned at her attack of vanity. She wasn't out to impress anyone with her looks.

When she returned to the kitchen, Lorrie was ready to leave. "I'll see you guys in the morning." She sailed out the door with a sly smile at Carey.

"Okay, gang," Carey said with fake cheer, "let's get supper on the table. Sophie, put Highway in the utility room and wash your hands. Wayne, you can fold napkins."

She gave them tasks while she placed bowls of salad on the table. When they were ready, Sophie clasped her hand, then Wayne's.

"I'll say the blessing."

Carey kept her head down and her eyes averted from their guest's. As Sophie blessed everyone important in her life, including Freeway and Highway, longing grew in Carey for things she couldn't express.

When the prayer ended, Sophie asked Wayne, "Are you going to live with us now?"

"I'm visiting for a few days while I get well." He flicked Carey a blue laser glance. "Your mom didn't think I could make it on my own."

"Does your leg hurt? Mom said you were giving some of your bones to Jenny McCallum."

"Bone marrow cells," Carey corrected. "The new cells will replace Jenny's old ones and make her well again."

"We hope," Wayne added. "Will we try again if these don't work?"

"Yes. If you're up to it."

His grin was rueful. "I'd do it."

"You're very brave," Sophie said solemnly, sounding so much like her mother that the grown-ups burst into laughter.

"Will you read me a story?"

Wayne glanced up from the farm-and-ranch magazine. Sophie stood across the living room, her gaze expectant. She was dressed in flannel pajamas with feet on them. She looked like a cherub.

"Sure."

She climbed into his lap, surprising him. He winced, then shifted her slight weight off his sore leg.

"Where's your mom?"

"Cleaning the bathroom. I splashed."

The simplicity of her explanation reached right inside him.

"Here's my book. It's my favorite."

He took the book and began. The story was about a bear family who lived in a tree house. He read the adventure, then he and Sophie discussed it in detail. He could see she was envious of the fun the bear brother and sister had.

"I had a younger brother," he told her. "It wasn't always fun. Sometimes he wanted to go with me, but I wanted to be with my friends."

She bobbed her head against his chest. "I know all about that. The bear brother and sister got in a fight in one book. Mama Bear didn't like it."

She told him the whole story in the most serious tone he could imagine. "It was like that with me and my brother at times," he said when she finished.

"But sometimes you liked him?"

"Yeah, sometimes."

He thought of Dugin, who'd been a pest. In 'Nam, he'd found himself thinking of the times they'd gone skinny-dipping, of the camp-outs and hikes, of the hunting trips that most often yielded nothing but companionship.

Regret hit him hard. He should have come back and checked on his younger brother. Maybe he could have saved his life. To die so uselessly—

"Tell Mr. Kincaid good-night," Carey ordered from across the room.

Wayne didn't need a crystal ball to see she was angry with him. He accepted the child's kiss and hug, then set her on her feet. "Don't forget your book." He handed it over.

Carey escorted her daughter down the hall. It was thirty minutes before she returned to the living room. He tensed when she came in.

"Did I do something wrong?" he asked, wanting to get to the bottom of this.

She pushed the tousled curls back from her temples. It was a gesture he'd seen her use when she was tired. "No. I didn't mean for Sophie to impose on you. I thought she'd gone to her room."

"It wasn't an imposition. I enjoyed reading the story to her."

He watched Carey struggle with words. Finally she spoke.

"I don't want her to get used to having you around. It was a mistake bringing you here."

"I didn't ask," he reminded her, his own temper rising.

"I know." A flush added becoming color to her cheeks.

His anger died as he noted how beautiful she was. The lamplight gleamed off the soft curls that surrounded her face. Her eyes held the purity of thought and purpose he'd seen depicted in paintings of the Madonna.

As he watched her, his feelings shifted from the spiritual to the carnal. In spite of the soreness in his body, desire stirred, as irrepressible as the pup he'd given Sophie. He wanted this woman in his arms, in his bed...

He felt like a string of barbed wire pulled too tight. An extra ounce of pressure and he'd snap. "I can leave tonight. Perhaps that would be best."

She shook her head. "It's too dangerous. It's supposed to snow. You could get stuck in a drift. Let's give it a couple of days and see how you feel."

"All right." He was willing. He realized he didn't want to leave this warm home and return to life in the bunkhouse.

"I think I'll light the fire." She added logs to the hearth, then started the fire with the practiced ease of a woman used to doing for herself. She left him with the flames lapping hungrily over the logs.

He closed his eyes and listened to the sounds of the wind outside the snug house and the woman moving about in the kitchen. There was peace to be found here. That could be dangerous to a man who didn't intend to stay.

In a few minutes, she brought mugs of hot, spiced cider into the room. She handed him two pills and a glass of water first. He took the pills without bothering to ask what they were. They each read a magazine as they sipped the cider.

"It's snowing," she said at one point.

He glanced toward the windows. The snow was coming down in thick clots that broke apart when they struck the glass. It was already a half inch thick on the sill.

"This will be hard on the cattle," he said.

"Yes."

He turned off the lamp beside his chair and watched the play of firelight over her face. Her sweat suit was faded to a gray-green color that took on bronzed touches as the flames leaped higher. Her hair and skin glowed.

She laid the magazine aside and let her head fall back against the sofa as she stared into the fire. It was as if they were cut off from the world at this moment.

He wanted it to last.

The rush of emotion caught him off guard. If he could have managed the feat, he'd have swept her into his arms and made the sweetest love to her. As it was, he could only watch and wish that life had been different, that somehow it could be kinder and gentler, as someone had once said.

But it was real and harsh and unforgiving.

"I'm going to bed," he said. "If you would point me in the direction?"

She leaped up as if startled out of a dream. "Of course. I should have…I mean, it's through here." She handed him the cane and led the way down the hall to a bedroom at the far end.

The room was cool after the warmth of the fire. He waited while she turned down the bed and laid an extra blanket out. She also had a pair of pajamas for him and a thick terry robe along with tube socks.

"My dad left the robe last time he was here," she explained. "Lorrie picked up the pajamas at the store. We guessed on the size. There are towels and razors and soap in the guest bathroom. It's next door."

"Thanks."

She scurried out.

Moving carefully, he undressed and pulled on the pjs. He brushed his teeth with a new toothbrush he found in the bathroom. She'd thought of everything.

Except that he couldn't sleep. The bed was too lonely and too cold after sharing hers. He lay there for an hour.

At last, need overcame common sense. He struggled out of bed and limped down the hall with the aid of the cane. At her door, he paused, then opened it. She was reading.

Her eyes were luminous as she stared across the room at him. He closed the door and limped to the other side of the wide bed. "I can't sleep down there," he explained.

He got in bed, sighed and closed his eyes. After a few minutes, she clicked off the light and lay down. After another minute, she moved over and laid her arm across his middle. Her leg touched his.

"That's better," he murmured. He thought of all the

reasons he shouldn't be doing this. "What the hell," he said, and looped an arm around her shoulders. He dropped into a deep, peaceful sleep.

Nine

Wayne opened his eyes at the scrape of the lock across the door frame. Dark hair surrounding an oval face appeared. Lorrie's dark eyes fastened on him. She stopped.

"Hi," he said.

A smile bloomed on her mouth. Her eyes took on a shine of wicked glee. "Well, hello."

He tried to think of an explanation for why he was in Carey's bed. He gave up. "Don't read anything into this," he advised gruffly. "It doesn't mean anything. That is, nothing happened."

She looked distinctly disappointed. "Too bad."

He realized he had an adult ally in the house. "Carey wouldn't agree with that assessment." He pushed himself upright very, very carefully. God, he could hardly move.

Lorrie handed him the cane.

"Thanks. This is worse than I thought." He gritted his teeth and headed for the bathroom. It wasn't until he was in the shower that he realized he probably should have gone to the guest bath down the hall.

He liked this one better. Carey's scent lingered in the close quarters. He inhaled deeply, smelling shampoo and soap and the lightly scented powder she used. He used her razor, then hobbled into the bedroom.

The bed was made and his clothing from yesterday, freshly washed and ironed, lay on the comforter. He dressed and hobbled to the guest bathroom to brush his teeth before heading for the kitchen for coffee.

Lorrie was there. She put his breakfast on the table. Looking out the window, he saw the snow was only two or three inches deep. Not enough to keep Montana folks from getting out and about their business. Certainly not enough to keep Carey home with him for the day. He ate the orange sections, then the pancakes and bacon.

"That was great, Lorrie. Thanks." He glanced at the clock. "Nine already?"

"You slept late. Carey is at her office. Sophie is at school. Sterling McCallum will be out to see you—"

The fire siren went off at the courthouse. It was a call for all volunteers to report to the firehouse on the double. He and Lorrie checked the kitchen windows, but couldn't see any smoke.

"My husband is a fireman," she said, a worried frown wrinkling her brow. "He's off duty—four days on, four days off is how they work. He just got off last night, but he'll have to go in for this one."

"Maybe it's nothing, a grass fire or something." He realized how stupid that sounded. A grass fire with snow on the ground? Hardly.

She turned on the radio.

"Fire at the Kincaid ranch," a reporter was saying. "We'll have a full report at ten."

Wayne sprang to his feet, then cursed as pain shot through his left hip. He grabbed the back of the chair. "I've got to get out there."

Lorrie pressed her lips together, then nodded. "I'll drive. We'll go in your truck." She tossed him his coat and pulled on a red-and-black parka. She grabbed a toboggan cap and looked at him.

"My hat is in the truck." He jerked on the shearling jacket and limped toward the garage a step behind Lorrie.

They headed for the Kincaid ranch. Two fire engines passed them on the way. The fire chief was there when they arrived. So was Judd Hensley, the sheriff, and Sterling McCallum, the sheriff's chief investigator.

The firemen wet down the ranch buildings while the hay barn burned to the ground, too far gone to save.

Rand Harding, cursing a blue streak until he spotted Lorrie standing next to Wayne, was directing the four hands in moving the nervous horses away from the area. The cattle milled and bawled in the home pastures, upset by the commotion.

The last standing wall of the barn collapsed with a groan of strained timbers and a great swirl of embers rushing up to the crystal-clear sky. The snow reflected the orange glow of the flames. Wayne watched impassively as the rest of the winter feed turned to ashes.

After the fire burned itself out, the firemen soaked the remains. Lorrie spoke to her husband, then asked if Wayne was ready to go back to town. If he was, her husband wanted a ride back to their house.

"I'll drop you off," Sterling told him. "The sheriff wants to talk to us."

Wayne told Lorrie and her husband to go on. He'd be in later. Leaning heavily on the cane, he led the way to the bunkhouse. There would be coffee on hand and a place to sit. He couldn't believe how tired his leg had gotten while he watched the fire eat up the rest of the Kincaid resources.

At the bunkhouse, he saw it was almost noon, and realized he'd been standing for over two hours. Carey would have his hide if she knew. Taking it easy? Right.

He checked the pot, found it full and helped himself. The sheriff and deputy did the same. Rand Harding came in. He washed up at the sink, then joined them.

"This cuts it," Rand said in disgust. "We'll have to sell out now. Hargrove was out here last week. He says Lester Buell has a buyer. You gonna contact him?" He glanced at the deputy, then stared at the cup of coffee in his hands.

Sterling shook his head. "I don't know. I'll have to go over everything with the bank and, of course, Hargrove, since he's the attorney for the estate."

Wayne rubbed his forehead, where a headache was

now ticking like a time bomb getting ready to go off. There was something... If he could just remember.

"You look as if you might have thought of something," the sheriff commented. "We could use a clue."

"Yeah. I do remember one thing. Rand reminded me when he mentioned Buell. Lester tried to buy the ranch once before. A long time ago."

The memory flooded in. Buell had been sniffing around the ranch about the time he'd caught his father in the hay with another man's wife, the day his mother had cried her heart out over a man who hadn't been worth a damn—

"Well?" Hensley broke in. "Is that it?"

He looked tired and impatient. McCallum didn't look too good, either. The vigil at the hospital was wearing him and his wife down.

Wayne nodded. "When I was a kid, the ranch went through a hard time, the usual thing—prices down, costs up. Buell came around then, too, trying to buy the ranch for a song. My dad threw him off the place, told him he'd shoot him if he ever showed up again."

"That was Jeremiah," Hensley said. A half smile flicked across his face.

Wayne remembered that his dad had once had friends and been a respected member of the community. A man's indiscretions were often overlooked and forgiven.

But *he* hadn't forgiven. He'd never forget his mother's tears, his own shock. His dad, the man he'd trusted more than anyone else in the world, had been a liar and a cheater.

"Yeah, but it was more than that. The old man was madder than a bent-tail bull about something else."

Wayne tried to let the thought come to the forefront. He couldn't quite grasp it, but there had been something about Buell's offer that had infuriated his father. It came to him.

"Buell was a front for someone else," he said. "He didn't have the money for a spread like this."

"Still doesn't," Sterling added. He took a drink of coffee, his eyes narrowed in thought.

"But I can't remember who it was. I think the old man figured it out, though. He was fit to be tied."

"Now Buell is nosing around again," Sterling murmured. "And things are happening on the ranch."

"You think Dale Carson is working for Buell?" the foreman asked. "You think he set fire to the barn? He must have done it. He would know the men and I were out at first light to check the cattle after the storm came through. We had six inches of snow in some spots."

"Carson is the prime suspect." Wayne spoke to Sterling. "You talked to Reed Austin lately? He was trying to get the information out of Janie Carson, I think."

Wayne felt his ears growing warm as he recalled the incident in the park with Janie. Carey had been furious. As if he'd pick the kid over a woman like her. She had a lot to learn if she thought that.

"Dale is down in Denver," Sterling reported. "Austin says Janie got a call from him the other day. He's got a job on a ranch there. I know where he is. I don't think he'll be going anyplace we can't find him if we need to."

"He isn't our man," Wayne said. "Buell flashed some bills in his face and he got greedy. Momentarily. I think nearly getting caught put the fear of jail in him. Buell, or whoever he's working for, has brought in someone else."

Sterling muttered an imprecation.

The sheriff stood. "I've got to get back to the office. You giving Kincaid a ride?" he asked Sterling.

"Yeah."

After they were on the road, Wayne spoke his mind to Sterling. "Buell is the lead to whoever wants the ranch."

"I think you're right."

"Can you put a tail on him? Maybe check his phone calls? He has a cell phone. I'd check that."

Sterling exhaled heavily. "I'd have to get a court order. It takes proof of wrongdoing, or at least a strong suspicion of it, enough to convince a judge."

"Probable cause." Wayne closed his eyes and sought the answer. He had the key. He knew he did. But it was locked into a fifteen-year-old's memories of his father and mother and a time that had been filled with disillusionment.

"Talk to Kate," he suggested.

"The hanging judge?" Sterling mocked. "She's the toughest one on the county circuit."

"She's fair."

"Yeah, she is. She'll listen, too. I'll tell her Buell is a front for someone, and that somebody is going to get killed if we don't stop these accidents at the ranch." His tone was full of irony and controlled anger. "If the fire doesn't do it, they might decide they need to get rid of all the heirs. Be careful."

Wayne's stomach clenched at the harsh truth of this statement. Moving a tractor, making ghostly noises and scaring the cattle were one thing. Men who would set fires and use poison were something else.

Dangerous. That was the word.

Sterling pulled into the drive at Carey's place. Wayne didn't even bother to ask how the deputy knew he was staying there. He had no doubt the local grapevine was alive and well in Whitehorn and would be as long as Lily Mae Wheeler lived there.

"Keep in touch," the lawman requested. "Let me know if you think of anything. I'll talk to Judd about going to Judge Walker."

Wayne nodded and climbed out of the vehicle with difficulty. His hip hurt like a toothache. His head throbbed in sympathy. He hobbled up to the door and tried the knob. It opened. He went inside.

The house was warm. The smell of something mouthwatering wafted from the kitchen. He headed that way. Lorrie was there, a spoon in hand, peering into a pot.

So was Carey. His heart twanged energetically.

She pinned him with her doctor glare. "Can't I take my eyes off you for a minute?" she demanded. "Come here and sit down. You've probably ripped your wound open."

"Lunch in two minutes," Lorrie announced calmly.

He hung his jacket and hat on a peg, then took a seat. Under the table, he rubbed his thigh as the pain seared the nerve endings like heat lightning. Carey thumped two pills and a glass of water on the table.

Without a word, he took the pills. Something that had been hard and tight within him eased up a bit. He breathed deeply and caught a whiff of Carey's enticing scent. Mixed with the aroma of stew and some kind of pie baking in the oven, it was almost enough to send him into ecstasy.

Lorrie served up three bowls of the stew and a basket of assorted crackers and crispbread. She removed a cobbler from the oven. Carey sat down opposite him.

The pain began to fade. By the time he finished the bowl of homemade mutton stew, he was feeling good. Watching Carey across the table, he began to feel other, less clearly defined, emotions. That made him uneasy. If they could solve the ranch problems, then he could leave.

Assuming Jenny was okay, of course.

Her eyes met his, cool as the under side of a pillow. "What happened at the ranch?"

"Someone burned the winter hay."

"Right after a storm?"

She looked so shocked and indignant his heart strummed again. "They were smart."

"Well, you can bring the cattle over to my place," she said, nodding decisively. "There must be three years' worth of hay on the ground. This snow will soon melt off and the cattle can get to it. Would that get you through the winter?"

"Yeah." His voice came out husky.

Her generous offer hit a spot that was tender in him. At the same time, desire thickened, sending a hot shaft of need pulsing through his body. What a fool that husband had been to give up a woman like her.

Realizing what he was thinking, he forcibly turned his thoughts to the two women and their conversation.

"Don't forget, the school play is next Friday," Lorrie reminded Carey. "You volunteered to bake scones and do the clotted cream again this year. She's a glutton for work," she added in an aside to him.

He nodded. A yawn overtook him.

"We'd better feed him and get him to bed," Carey suggested dryly. "Would you like milk with your cobbler?"

"Coffee."

"No coffee," she said firmly.

"If I didn't have a choice, why did you ask?" he demanded, not at all annoyed, but feeling compelled to assert his independence against this female barrage.

"You may have water if you don't want milk."

He knew when to give in gracefully. "Milk."

She beamed a smile his way. "Good boy."

Lorrie laughed as if this were the funniest thing in the world. Carey did, too. Women were strange creatures.

The housekeeper checked the calendar. "Sophie can eat with us tonight. I'll take her to the play practice along with my granddaughter. I can drop her off when practice is over, probably around eight."

Carey spooned up the cobbler. "That would be good. I want to stop by the hospital and check Jenny McCallum."

"Any word on the transplant?" he asked.

"Not yet. We're watching for allergic reactions."

"I hope it takes." He rubbed his leg and managed a rueful smile.

"Don't we all," Lorrie declared.

Carey served the cobbler, along with milk for him and herself. Lorrie got to have coffee with hers, but he didn't ask why.

"You need the calcium," Carey said, reading his mind. "And the protein. And a nap after lunch."

"Okay, I'm not complaining. This is the best cobbler I've ever had."

"An old family recipe. I'll give it to you."

"Yeah, thanks." He felt a tug at the corners of his mouth as she grinned at him. "You're feeling frisky today."

"She's like this when things go well with a patient," Lorrie warned. "You'd better watch out. She'll have you up dancing the watusi before you know it."

Carey laughed, a surprisingly young sound. With her smooth complexion and tousle of curls, she looked hardly older than her daughter. He suddenly remembered times when his mother had laughed. And that she'd loved to dance.

He'd once caught her and his father dancing very close and very suggestively when he'd been a youngster. It had excited and embarrassed him at the same time. When he'd grown knowledgeable in the ways of men and women, he'd realized why.

The mating instinct. It was an elemental driving force between the sexes.

Carey glanced at him, found him staring and stopped smiling. Her pupils expanded to blot the complex hazel flecks from her eyes, making them appear dark and mysterious.

Silence reigned as the older woman straightened up the kitchen and prepared to leave. She covertly studied them while she wrapped up to brave the cold. "See you later," she told them, and left.

Carey stood, too. "I have to go."

"Now?" He couldn't stifle the disappointment. His thoughts had been drifting toward bed and a nap. Maybe a nap, but definitely bed.

"Patients, lots of them this afternoon. It's cold and flu season." She washed her hands and rubbed in lotion.

His skin flushed as he remembered those ultrasmooth fingers touching his flesh. He pushed himself upright with an effort. Forgetting the cane, he hobbled over to her.

"Then I need this to get me through the day."

He put his arms around her, half expecting protest, in which case he'd argue. He hoped it wouldn't be an outright refusal. He didn't want to hear no from her.

Her eyes widened, but she didn't say a word. She laid her hands on his chest, but didn't push away. She lifted her face to his and watched as he leaned down to her.

He felt her sigh just before his lips settled over hers. Need beat through him like a mad drummer in ecstasy. He adjusted his body to fit her curves, using his greater weight to press her against the cabinet. He wished he could lift her to the counter, but that would have to wait for another time.

She rocked against him, her arms sliding up and over his shoulders. Strength poured into him when he felt the sensual imprint of her breasts and stomach and thighs against his. She made little sounds that drove him to fever pitch.

He moved against her, tucking his thigh between hers and rubbing insistently, until she clutched at his shirt, as desperate for him as he was for her.

"Stay," he whispered.

"I can't."

"An hour."

"Umm…no…really…."

He cupped her breasts and nuzzled them through her shirt until they formed hard beads against his mouth. She gasped and held on tighter.

"Come home early." He let her go and stepped back.

Her face was flushed a becoming rose. He almost drew her back into his arms. Instead, he took a breath and let it out with a calming whoosh.

"You drive me right to the edge," he muttered, not sure he liked a woman having this much control of his life.

"Me, too," she said, a bit glumly. She tucked the loose edges of her shirt in. "I'll probably see you around seven or eight. I might pick up Sophie."

"Coward."

She shook her head and her curls bounced, enticing him to run his fingers through them. He did under the pretext of smoothing them into place.

"An affair between us would be foolish." She retrieved her bulky sweater and her purse, which was big

enough to carry a full pack of surgical instruments...
and no doubt did.

A sense of tenderness tugged at him again, and again
he was surprised by it. She looked around for her
gloves.

He opened the drawer and pulled out a pair, holding
them while she slipped them on.

"Thank you." She found her keys and dashed out as
if the devil were on her heels.

With a wry chuckle, he limped down the hall to the
bedroom—her bedroom—and shucked his pants. He
climbed in and went to sleep before he'd more than reg-
istered her scent on the pillow next to his.

Carey studied Jenny's pink cheeks in alarm. A fever
could indicate her body was throwing off the marrow
cells instead of accepting them. Or it could mean the
child was coming down with an infection.

"She's looking better," Jessica said. "I think she's
livelier than she's been in a week."

Carey didn't glance at the hopeful mother. "Wait
until next month," she said in a light tone. "We'll have
to tie her to an anchor to keep her in one place."

Jenny gave her a faint smile.

Carey hooked the chart on the door, then washed her
hands and put on rubber gloves. Through sealed
openings on the bubble, she examined Jenny, checking
the lymph glands for signs of swelling. She swallowed
against tears. The child was so thin she could see the
damned glands and trace every vein under the pale skin.

Last, she took the temperature and read the digital number that appeared. One hundred and one.

She silently said an imprecation. Hiding all emotion, she tickled Jenny's feet. The child moved slightly and frowned at her. Carey smiled, chucked her under the chin as a reminder of her "chin up" lecture and withdrew her hands.

"You're looking good, kid," she assured both the patient and the mother. "Dr. Hunter will be in later. I didn't find any swelling, so that's good. She is running a fever, but that's not unusual."

After telling Jessica good-night and checking on two other youngsters, she left the hospital and walked through the slush to her vehicle. At her house, she pulled into the garage and sat in there in the dusk before climbing wearily out. The scent of stew greeted her when she walked in.

The table was already laid for two.

"Hi, you're just in time," Wayne said.

She blinked warily. She trusted a domesticated wolf even less than she did a wild one.

"You look very much at—if you'll forgive the pun—home on the range." She allowed herself one sardonic smile.

He cocked his head and studied her for a long twenty seconds. "You're tired. Change clothes, then it'll be time to eat."

She sniffed at his order, but carried it out. When she returned to the kitchen, she found warm bread in a basket on the table and the bowls filled with stew. A glass of milk was at each place.

"You're supposed to be the patient," she told him, slipping into the seat. "Did you rest this afternoon?"

"Yes, ma'am. After those knockout pills you gave me, I snoozed like a baby all afternoon."

"Good."

The conversation lapsed after that. Strangely, she didn't feel uncomfortable with the silence.

She watched him for a while. He was handsome in a rough kind of way, with nothing of the smooth, flawless boy about him now. Well, of course not. Twenty-five years would make a difference in anyone's looks. Still, she'd seen men who remained what she termed as "smoothies" even as they grew old. Her husband was such a man. He always had a smile and looked like a million.

The telephone rang just as she finished. She was up and across the room before her guest could move. "Hello."

"This is Kane."

Her heart sank. "You've seen Jennifer?"

"Yeah. I see you started her on one of the new antibiotics. Good thinking. It's usually well tolerated in cases like this."

"You think it's an infection, then?"

He sighed. "It's fifty-fifty right now. It could be a bug…or rejection."

She heard the quiet seriousness in his tone. "That's what I thought. I'll stop by in the morning."

"Good. How's our other patient doing?"

She glanced at Wayne. "Fine. Thanks for calling." She hung up, then stood there staring out at the twilight.

Jenny had nothing left in her body to fight infection except the intense heat of fever. If an infection took hold, it would be hard to stop. Carey's shoulders slumped. She'd faced death before. And been beat by it.

A warm arm draped over her shoulders. "Tell me."

She stared at the man who'd once been the golden boy of the county and shook her head. "I was remembering..."

"What?"

"In ten years, since I entered medical school and started actually seeing life and death, I've lost four patients. The first time I went into a frenzy of study. I read everything I could find on the disease for months. Then I went over every treatment I'd tried. I thought there had to be an answer. That if I had worked harder, longer, done something differently, I could have made it work."

"But you couldn't have."

She shook her head. "The chief resident took me aside one day. He sat me down in a corner of the children's playroom and made me look at all those kids. He pointed out one little boy and told me he was going to die. He said the same about another. He said he couldn't save them, that he wasn't God. He asked me if I could."

"Is this about Jenny?"

She nodded, opened her mouth, closed it, swallowed, then nodded again. The hot ball of tears stuck in her throat, making speech impossible. She pressed her forehead against his chest and closed her eyes.

"Make love to me," she said after a while.

"It might not be wise. You're hurting."

She was. Everywhere. His warmth helped. She wanted more. Lifting her head, she kissed him. For a second, she sensed his hesitation, then his muscles tightened, and he answered the kiss. The passion escalated.

She rubbed against him, sensuous as a cat, demanding fulfillment, needing him in a way she hadn't let herself need another being in a long time. Fire spread through her, thawing all the cold, angry places where logic couldn't reach. Her body softened, yielding to the desire.

He slid his hands over her, down her hips, catching her and bringing her into hard contact with the rigid staff of his need. She reacted instinctively, lifting one leg to entwine with his, melding them closer, moving against him in a primal rhythm.

After an eternity, he set her away. Their breaths came quickly. She returned the searching look he gave her, not backing down as his eyes questioned.

"I want you," she said softly.

"All right, then."

Together, without need for more words, they walked down the hallway and into her bedroom. Her hands, quick, capable and efficient, moved over him, then herself, as she removed their clothing. They kissed, then somehow— she never knew exactly when—they fell into bed.

"You'll have to do the riding tonight," he murmured, a quick smile lighting his face for an instant.

"Yes, but first, I want to feel you all over, with my entire body."

"Have it your way." His smile teased, but his tone was serious, almost as if they exchanged vows.

If they did, only their hearts knew the words. Neither spoke aloud of feelings, but a certainty grew in her—that this was right, that it was okay to care, that she could trust again....

She lay so that they touched all over, her head next to his on the pillow. "Does this make you uncomfortable? Any pain?"

He grinned in that slow way he had that stirred her senses and her heart. "Only the one of wanting you."

She gazed into his eyes, so blue, so easy to drown her worries in and forget tomorrow. He'd said he would be leaving soon. Part of her was sure he wouldn't.

However, he hadn't made any promises. If she just remembered that, she would be okay. She would make sure Sophie knew it, too.

When he cupped her hips, then began a slow rhythmic stroking over her back and sides, the flame burned out the last cautious thought on a future with this man.

His kisses imprinted her soul and fed her hunger for more of his taste. She repeated his restless movements until they were both hot and gasping. When she could stand it no longer, she pushed upright and took him into her.

"Ah, love," he whispered, his hands moving, searching, finding her most sensitive spots. "Carey, my love."

Her world, which had come perilously close to shattering earlier, locked tightly into one solid sphere in that instant—whole, complete, fulfilled.

Ten

Jennifer McCallum's temperature hit 105 and stayed there. Carey ordered cool baths and consulted with Kane and the cancer specialist on fever-reducing medications and methods.

They had to be extra cautious. Jenny's young life was in the balance, and everyone in the town knew it. The one time Carey took a few minutes to stop at the café for lunch, her presence produced an immediate and deadly quiet as the local folks looked at her, a question in their eyes.

She shook her head to tell them there was no change.

At home, Lorrie and Wayne and Sophie made life easy on her. Meals were prepared when she arrived each day. She and Sophie made the scones for the school play, while Wayne watched them with a smile that seemed tender, yet serious.

Each night, she turned to him, needing the haven of his arms and the drugging effect of their tempestuous lovemaking to fall asleep. Even then, she often stirred restlessly, unable to relax. Once, she awoke to find him rubbing her back and neck, his voice a low, rough croon as he spoke softly, telling her to sleep.

A week sped by, with the days blurring together as her workload increased. On Friday, Carey was up and dressed before the sun was above the horizon. She'd planned to take the day off to help with the school play, but her patients' needs were too pressing as a new virus made the rounds.

At noon, Wayne appeared at the office. He carried a large brown bag. "Time to eat," he announced. "When does she get a lunch break?" he asked the nurse.

"There are four more morning appointments yet," she said.

Carey wrinkled her nose at him. "Thanks for lunch. Just leave it on my desk. I'll get to it—"

The next thing she knew she was hauled into her office and the door firmly closed. He pushed in the lock.

"Sit," he ordered. He plunked a take-out container on the desk and kept one for himself.

Inside she found the Hip Hop's famous barbecued chicken and baked beans. She inhaled deeply. "Umm, heavenly." She ate ravenously and cleared her plate in ten minutes flat.

He eyed her in exasperation.

"What?" she asked.

"Hasn't your doctor ever talked to you about slowing down and enjoying life?"

"Doctors don't have time for doctors."

"Very funny." He glared at her. When he finished, he pushed the chair back and invited her into his lap.

"Only for a minute," she said, glancing at the clock.

"Shut up." He leaned her against his arm, then proceeded to ravish her with his mouth and his hands.

Long before the minute was up, she knew she'd made a mistake. She wanted more than kisses and soft touches. She wanted…

The answer came to her with the swiftness of a light-bulb clicking on. She wanted this man in her life.

For more than a day. Or a night. For more than a week or a month. For as long as…no, don't think it.

She pulled back from the kiss and struggled to her feet. He let her go, but didn't help her up.

"What dark thought entered your mind?" he asked.

"Nothing. I really have to go."

"Are you going to make the play?"

"Yes. I told Lorrie I'd meet her and Sophie at the school at seven."

"Will you?" He gave her a piercing glance. "You haven't been home before eight this week."

"I know, but things have gotten hectic lately."

He studied her another few seconds, then nodded. He walked to the door.

"You aren't using the cane today. Your limp is gone. That's good." She smiled approvingly.

"Save your doctor's smile for those who need it," he said sarcastically, and walked out.

She stiffened at the sudden attack. A glance from the nurse had her heading down the hall to the examining room. She had patients to worry about.

It was almost six when she locked the side door behind her and ran toward her ute. She almost crashed into a shadowy figure coming up the sidewalk. "Oh."

"It's me," the figure in an odd assortment of winter clothing told her. Wild gray hair stuck out from a black knitted cap. A long, shapeless beard hung down to his chest.

She recognized Kane's father-in-law, Homer Gilmore. The town's beloved old eccentric lived upstairs during the colder months and went prospecting in the summer. "Good evening," she said. "Gotta dash. There's a school play tonight."

"You'd better watch it," he said. "Strange things go on around here all the time."

A chill rustled up the hairs on her neck. She thought of Wayne and the fire at the ranch and stopped. "Did you see someone start the fire at the Kincaid ranch?"

"No, nothing like that, but tell Kincaid to beware of weasels in the henhouse."

She stifled her disappointment. She'd hoped the old man might have some information she could give Sterling and Reed Austin, who'd been assigned to work with the deputy chief.

"Thanks. I will. See you later."

"It's outsiders that's doing it," he called after her as she rushed down the slippery sidewalk to her ute.

She smiled. At least he'd stopped blaming aliens for all the strange happenings in the county. Glancing at the digital clock on the radio, she saw she didn't have time to go home and change. She would go see Jenny, then dash over to the school for the play. No time for supper, either. So what else was new? She eased out onto the street and drove to the hospital.

For a moment, she thought of Wayne and the lunch he'd brought in. That had been thoughtful.

He'd been at her house since the transplant, except for daily excursions to the ranch, and she'd found him wonderful in many ways.

As a guest he was charming, easily winning Lorrie's and Sophie's loyalty. He had shown Sophie how to house-train Highway in an afternoon.

As a lover, he was exciting, sensual and sensitive to her desires. Each time she thought of their lovemaking, wild sensations rioted through her, making her tremble. She shied from thinking of the future. There was today. That was all she could afford to think about at the present.

She parked and hurried inside the hospital.

"Where is your coat?" Annie demanded when she paused by the desk.

"In the car. I'm only here for a minute. I wanted to check…" She forgot the rest of the sentence as she looked over Jenny's chart. She quickly walked down the corridor to the quarantine section.

Jessica was reading a book. Jenny was asleep. The

bloom of fever had faded from her cheeks. A light sheen of perspiration gleamed on the child's face. Carey looked at the temperature recordings and breathed a thankful prayer.

After speaking to Jessica, she donned gloves and skimmed her hands over the sleeping child.

"It's broken," she said at last. She blinked as unexpected tears surged into her eyes. "Jessica, the fever is broken."

The young mother tossed her book down and stood beside Carey, both of them watching Jennifer. Carey withdrew her hands. She smiled. Two fat tears cascaded down her face.

Jessica, also teary eyed, threw her arms around Carey. They hugged each other wordlessly, sharing the moment as parents and friends.

"She's going to be all right," Jessica said in wonder, sniffing as they recovered their composure. "She is, isn't she? Doesn't this mean she's going to be all right?"

"If the marrow cells take," Carey reminded her.

Wayne guided his truck into the parking place and killed the engine. His breath made a puff of frost in front of his face as he climbed out and walked carefully over the rough, icy surface of the parking lot to the schoolhouse.

Inside, he glanced all around, nodding here and there to people he recognized. Austin Reed was with Janie Carson. Reed grinned, obviously happy with the way things were working out, while Janie gave him a cool nod.

The young woman was one person who would never think well of him, he mused as he took a chair and put his jacket in the next one to save it for Carey. If she got there.

He pondered his irritation with her and admitted he'd wanted her to forget everything but him after lunch.

A tap on his shoulder drew his attention. The sheriff and his family were present. He shook hands with Tracy and met a little girl. The baby boy grabbed his finger and tried to chew on it.

"Teething," Tracy said, smiling as she substituted a rubber ring for his finger.

One minute before the play began, he saw Carey rush in and look around. He motioned to her and moved his jacket.

Her warm smile flooded her face. She looked at ease for the first time that week. She slipped down the aisle and slid in next to him. As usual, she wore her bulky cardigan and had left her coat in the ute. Her hands were bare. She'd lost two pairs of gloves that week.

She tucked her fingers under her arms. "Cold out there." She leaned close. "Jenny's fever has broken." She leaned over the back of the seat to the Hensley family. "Jennifer McCallum's fever has broken."

"Lily Mae Wheeler is one aisle over," he told her with a sardonic grin.

"Lily Mae," Carey called to catch the town gossip's attention. "Jenny McCallum's temperature is down to normal."

"The fever has broken?" the woman asked, her

earrings, great gold loops within loops, swinging wildly. Her carmine lips split into a dazzling smile of capped teeth. "The little darling is going to be all right?"

"Well, if the transplant takes," Carey hedged, her gaze becoming pensive.

Wayne took her hand and squeezed it, then rubbed it to bring the warmth back. "It will," he said, setting his jaw and daring fate to snatch victory from this woman who worked so hard and cared so much. "It will."

Beside him, she sighed and murmured, "I hope so."

The curtains opened and the play began. Afterward, they all had watery punch and goodies baked by harried mothers. The scones disappeared first.

Wayne looked around and saw families laughing and chatting in every corner of the gym. He watched Carey hug her daughter and tell her how great she'd been.

A strange warmth flowed through him. For a moment, he imagined being part of a real family, the kind the sheriff shared with his wife and kids.

A sensation like a cold wind down his neck told him he should have left weeks ago. He wouldn't be here now if not for his little sister—another victim of his father's lascivious ways.

The painful memories rushed at him, reminding him of all the reasons he'd left twenty-five years ago. He'd grown used to the freedom of the road. He wasn't a settling-down kind of man—

Sophie ran to him and hugged his leg. "Did you see me?" she demanded. "Did you like my song?"

He swung her up to his shoulders. "I sure did. You were very nearly the best one on the stage."

She giggled happily and patted his head. "Look, Mom, look how big I am up here!"

Wayne awoke at first light. He lay in bed and listened to the morning sounds—the caw of a crow in the distance, the rumble of a truck a couple of streets over, the whisper of the wind through the trees.

At the ranch, he would have heard the lowing of cattle along with the birds and the wind, maybe the rumble of a tractor pulling a hay wagon into the fields.

Except there would be no tractor and hay wagon now. They were down to the last rolls of hay on the ranch.

He turned over on his side, cupping his body to Carey's, and inhaled the warm, sleepy scent of woman. "You awake already?"

"Umm-hmm." She drew his arm across her body and snuggled into him, causing a ripple of hunger to pass through him.

"What are your plans for the day?" he asked.

"I need to go by the hospital, then the office for Saturday-morning appointments. What about you?"

He hesitated. "I have to return to the ranch. It's time I got back to work. We'll start moving cattle over to your place this afternoon. I won't be here when you get back."

She didn't protest. However, after planting a kiss on his shoulder, she sighed. Her next words pleased him.

"All good things must come to an end, I suppose. Sophie is going to Lorrie's this afternoon to play with her granddaughter. I'd like to go along on the trail. Do you have a horse I could ride, one that's old and decrepit and won't buck?"

He raised up on an elbow to study her. "You sure? It'll make your backside pretty sore."

"Sore as hell," she correctly interpreted, drawing a laugh from him.

"You got that right." He patted her behind. "I'll give you a massage and a rubdown at your cabin. Why don't we stay the night there?"

"Sophie and I are already committed to Lorrie's for dinner. We're going to learn to make tortillas."

He swung out of bed, pulled on jeans and padded into the kitchen to see if the coffeemaker's timer had worked. It had. He poured them each a cup and went back to the bedroom, joining Carey, who was propped up on the pillows. He handed her the mug and slipped back under the warm covers.

"Thanks. Did I tell you I saw Homer Gilmore last night when I was leaving the office?"

"I don't recall you mentioning it."

"He said you should beware, that there are outsiders causing the problems at the ranch, but he didn't know who."

Wayne gave a snort. "As if we didn't know that." He leaned over and nuzzled her neck, smiling as she squirmed. She was ticklish below her ear, on her sides and her feet.

When he captured her mouth, he took the kiss deep. He heard the plunk of the mug when she set it on the nightstand, then felt her hands stroke through his hair as she responded fully to his embrace.

He caressed her hips, sneakily pulling her gown upward with each touch. When he had it out of the way, he moved over her, sliding between her thighs, feeling her move to accommodate him. He held himself in position, but instead of entering her, he caressed the passionate bud, feeding his desire and hers until, with a moan, she twisted her hips and thrust upward, sheathing him in her sweet warmth.

That was the invitation he'd been waiting for. He let himself glide slowly into the hot depths until they meshed completely. They both watched as he began the ancient rhythm of mating. He took her hand and guided it to the point of her passion, then supported himself on both hands while he moved deeply in her.

They exploded as one in a tense uncoiling of hunger that could be satisfied for the moment but never appeased. He lay beside her a long time before he had the energy to head for the shower.

When she joined him under the running water, he found he wasn't quite as exhausted as he thought.

The doorbell rang while Sophie, Carey and Wayne were finishing breakfast. Sterling McCallum removed his hat and asked for Wayne when Carey answered. She led the way to the kitchen, where she poured him a cup of coffee while the men exchanged greetings.

"How about a short stack of pancakes?" Carey asked. "They'll be thrown out if you don't eat them."

Sterling hesitated all of one second. "Well, if they're going to go to waste…" He took a seat at the table.

"Mom, can I play with Highway now?" Sophie asked.

"Yes, but dress first. Warm clothes. It's cold out today. And don't forget to put on extra socks."

"I won't."

Sophie gave her an indignant glare before rushing to let Highway out of the utility room and romping with him down the hall with the boisterous energy of youth. Both girl and dog were growing as fast as bean sprouts.

Glancing at the calendar, Carey realized it was the last day of February. Spring was right around the corner. She glanced at Wayne and wondered if he would be there when the new season arrived.

"What brings you out?" Wayne asked, changing from talk of the weather when the lawman finished.

"We got a trace on Buell's cell telephone. You ever heard of a guy named John Widdermann?"

Wayne thought it over. "No, it doesn't ring a bell."

Sterling sighed. "I thought for sure that would be a lead. Well, we're going to check the guy out, find out where he works and see if that makes a connection."

"Good. Sorry I can't help, but I'm still drawing a blank on whoever wanted the ranch before."

"There might not be a connection. There're enough scoundrels in the world to have more than one to a place."

The men exchanged sardonic glances.

Sterling turned to Carey. "Jessica thinks Jenny is better. She seems livelier than she has in days. Jessica is looking a little peaked, though."

"I'll be going to the hospital this morning. I'll check both of them out." She stood and touched Wayne's shoulder. "I'll join you at the ranch around one. How will I find you?"

"You'll see the trail of five hundred cattle easily. I'll ride drag until you catch up. Smoky will be your mount. We'll leave him in the corral."

She nodded, said goodbye to both men, pulled on her sweater and looked for her gloves. She frowned as she checked her pockets and the shelf above the telephone.

Wayne opened a drawer and gave her a know-it-all grin. She poked his belly, grabbed a pair and left.

On the street to the hospital, she pondered the morning and the strangely intense lovemaking they'd shared. A premonition stabbed her heart.

Wayne Kincaid, once the mystery of the ranch was solved, would have no reason to stay in Whitehorn. He would probably be gone with the spring thaw, moving on to greener pastures…and other women, she forced herself to add.

She closed her mind to the future while she parked and ran across the pavement to the ER entrance. No use borrowing trouble. She would face whatever had to be faced when the time came. She went straight to the lab.

"Well?" she demanded.

The lab technician gazed at her solemnly.

Her heart thudded to her toes.

Then he smiled. "She's making cells on her own. The transplant took," he told her. "By damn, it worked."

"Oh, my God." She clamped a hand over her mouth.

"Oh, my God," she said again. A smile spread over her face. "I've got to tell Jessica. Have you seen her?"

"Not yet. We just got the results."

"I'll find her. She'll want to tell Sterling."

Jessica was sitting beside the plastic bubble, reading a story to her daughter, when Carey paused at the door. Kane was with her. Annie saw them from the nursing station, took one look at their smiles and ran to join them.

"Good news," Carey said. She pointed at Jenny. "This girl is making blood cells on her own." She beamed a smile at the patient, then the mother. "The transplant worked."

"Dear God," Jessica said, her eyes going wide.

Carey and Kane laughed. Jessica and Annie burst into tears. Jennifer cried with them until Jessica assured the child they were crying because they were happy.

"When does she get out of the bubble? When can we take her home?"

Carey consulted with Kane.

"Tomorrow we take her out of the bubble," he said.

"She can go home at the end of the next week," Carey told Jessica. "But no going out for another six weeks. Don't let anyone with any sign of a sniffle in the house."

"No one will get in," Jessica vowed, looking so fierce they all laughed again. "Oh, I've got to tell Sterling."

She dashed to the telephone and dialed the dispatcher, who patched her through to his truck phone.

When Carey left the hospital, she was feeling good.

After a half day at the office, she headed home to change and see if Lorrie and Sophie had left yet.

At the house, the housekeeper was putting sheets in the dryer. "Hi, you're in earlier than I expected."

"Things were quiet at the office for a change. We got the report on Jennifer McCallum. The transplant took."

"Thank God for that." Lorrie wiped the tears that sprang to her eyes. "That must be why the deputy lit out of here with his lights flashing."

Carey told the housekeeper about going to the ranch for the cattle drive that afternoon. "But don't tell Sophie. I'd like some time on my own. You can reach me on the cell phone if anything comes up."

"Good," Lorrie said, a matchmaking gleam in her eye. "Why don't you let Sophie spend the night at my place? My granddaughter can stay, too. That way, my daughter can have some quiet time with the new baby."

Carey considered. "Let me talk to Sophie first. I like to keep my weekends for her. Is she in her room?"

"Yes. She was trying to teach Highway to color, but he ate the crayon. She's decided to teach him to sit up."

Sophie was delighted with the prospect of staying with Lorrie and her granddaughter. "This is my second sleepover," she announced, as if it were a great feat.

They packed an overnight case, ate lunch, then played until Lorrie was ready to leave.

After waving goodbye, Carey pulled on thermal long johns and jeans before heading for the Kincaid place. Her heart beat faster as she approached the ranch.

She'd been there for the wedding of Dugin Kincaid

to Mary Jo Plummer—actually Lexine Baxter, but no one knew that at the time—a few years ago. She could vaguely recall what the Kincaid house had looked like inside. Decorating didn't interest her. However, it was a shame no one lived in the mansion now.

The horse, Smoky, was in the corral as promised. She clipped a fanny pack of food and water around her waist and tied her first-aid kit behind the saddle. A cowboy hat was hung on the saddle horn. Under it was a note that told her to head due west past the old apple orchard. She put on the hat, opened the gate and started out.

An hour of steady riding brought her within hearing of the herd. She pulled the hat snug on her head and urged Smoky into a lope. In a few minutes, she joined them.

"Hi." Wayne rode up. "Any trouble finding us?"

She shook her head, letting her eyes roam his lean masculine figure. He was a handsome man in the saddle, seated astride an ebony gelding of part-Arabian stock.

"Did you remember to eat lunch?" he asked.

"You're turning into a nanny," she warned with a happy laugh. "Lorrie asks me that nearly everyday."

In truth, he made her feel cherished—a thing she'd never experienced from a man. Her heart bumped around in loopy circles in her chest as she let herself bask in the warm enchantment of his smile.

Longing rose in her. She wanted…she didn't know what. How much simpler life was for a child. She and Sophie had discussed the merits of brothers and sisters recently. Sophie wanted one of each. And a dog for each of them, too.

"How many puppies does Freeway have?" she called.

Wayne swung a rope and shooed some cows into line. He and the gelding fell back into step with her and Smoky. "There were four in the litter."

"So there are three left?"

"Yeah. I thought Sophie and I might take one to Jenny. If you think it will be okay. Maybe we could smuggle it up to the hospital and let her see it."

Her smile went radiant. "Better than that. You can take the pup to her house. She'll go home next week."

"Home," he repeated. "You mean…" He stared at her, hope and disbelief in his expression.

"The transplant took, yes."

She was jerked forward, almost falling off the horse, except there was a broad chest to catch her. She was very thoroughly kissed before he let her go. She sank into the saddle, her breathing fast.

"That's great news." His smile flashed over his tanned face, changing his appearance to one that was gentler. "I've been meaning to talk to Sterling about an idea for the ranch. You, too."

"Me?"

"You have the slopes on your land to make some fine ski runs. The Kincaid spread would be suitable for a vacation spot. With a golf course in addition to swimming, riding and hiking, the ranches could turn into a year-round resort and still run a cattle operation."

She blinked at him in amazement. "You have been doing some thinking." She considered the possibilities.

At the moment, nothing seemed impossible or too far-fetched for her to contemplate. "That's a wonderful idea. The remains of the old mining town, up where Homer was kept captive by Lexine, would be a great draw, too. We could renovate it and have parties in the saloon."

"After a hayride."

"Oh, yes. We could have horse rides along the ridge crest trail up to Crazy Mountain, too."

For the rest of the afternoon, she planned activities she thought vacationers would like. Until she noticed the laughter in his eyes. She tried to swat him with the borrowed hat, but he and his horse were too quick. They shied away in an effortless display of horsemanship.

It was almost dark before they galloped into the clearing in front of the Baxter cabin. He dismounted first, then came to her. Hands at her waist, he lifted her from the saddle as if she weighed nothing.

"How long have we got?" he asked.

"All night. Lorrie invited Sophie to spend the night with her."

Flames darted through his eyes. "I'll take care of the animals," he said. "It's getting too cold to be out."

She rushed inside, started the stove to warm up the cabin, then washed up and changed to sweats she'd left there the last time she'd visited. She unrolled two sleeping bags and laid them on the bunks.

Excitement rushed through her as she worked, making her want to laugh. She was happy, truly happy. Wayne came in on a rush of cold mountain air. She gave him a resounding kiss before removing the food she'd brought with her.

Later, sitting in his lap in front of the stove before going to bed, she sighed contentedly. As much as she loved her child, Sophie's sweet laughter and youthful enthusiasms weren't enough to fill the lonely corners of her life. For that, she needed an adult, someone who could be strong for her when she needed a shoulder to lean on after being strong for her patients all day.

Snuggled against Wayne's broad chest, replete from their lovemaking, she pitted the past against the future. Three years ago, in the aftermath of divorce, her child and her career had taken precedence. She'd thought they would be enough. But that was then.

It was time she reevaluated her goals. Longing rose in her, hot and aching and needful. A companion in life, that's what she wanted. Someone to love, freely and completely. Someone who would be there for her just as she would be there for him.

She knew who that someone was.

Eleven

The problem with even a short, one-day vacation, Carey decided on Monday morning, was having to go back to work. She stretched and threw off the covers. She'd slept okay, but it had been different without Wayne's long, sinewy length to keep her warm.

He'd stayed at the ranch yesterday while she came home to have Sunday with Sophie. He hadn't appeared last night, although she'd stayed up until eleven waiting for him.

He would be busy with the cattle until things were resolved at the ranch. And when they were?

She didn't have an answer.

The weekend had left her confused and wary. Not that she was confused about her feelings. Fact was fact. She'd fallen in love with Wayne Kincaid. She just didn't know what to do about it.

She'd relegated him to the role of drifter, a renegade without commitment to anyone, but knowing his true identity made a difference. Some part of her couldn't believe he'd walk away from his heritage again. Even if he didn't want to claim it, surely he wouldn't just leave.

That's where the confusion came in. She had no idea what he would do. And so she was wary. She had to guard her heart and that of her daughter, who asked about Wayne first thing when she got up that morning.

Carey and Sophie had breakfast together, then left. She dropped the girl at kindergarten, then went to the hospital. Jessica was waiting for her in Jenny's room.

Jenny looked tearful. The lab technician had just been in for a blood sample.

"How long will she have to be tested?" Jessica asked. "It seems ungrateful to ask, but she's so tired of needles."

"I know." Carey explained that they had to keep an eye on the blood count so they would know Jenny's new marrow was performing as it should. "She'll come in once a month for a while after she goes home, then once every three months, then once a year for a checkup as usual."

Jessica smiled in relief. "Jenny wants Sophie to come over and play with her when she goes home. Do you think it would be okay? I was thinking you might come for dinner Saturday night if you're not too busy."

"That sounds fine. As long as Jenny doesn't get overly tired, her activities should return to normal."

They talked about the weather—more snow on the way—and Jenny's care for the next few months. Carey saw the rest of her patients, then went to the office.

Moriah Hunter, who managed the office for her husband and Carey, stuck her head around the connecting door when Carey arrived. "My father said to tell you the outsiders aren't as pure as their name. Does that make any sense?"

Carey nodded. "He warned me about outsiders causing the problems at the Kincaid ranch. Lester Buell has made an offer for the ranch. Wayne and Sterling are sure he's acting for someone, but he won't say who. I'll tell Wayne what your father said. It might mean something more to him."

"It would be odd not to have the Kincaid ranch. The place has been a landmark in the county for so long."

"Sometimes a change is best," Carey said, echoing something Wayne, in his alter ego of J. D. Cade, had once said to her.

However, those had been words spoken by a man who had denied his past for twenty-five years. He would have to come to grips with it before he could find the peace he needed to settle in one place and build a life.

"Are they going to sell?"

Carey shrugged and tossed her purse and cardigan on the credenza in her office. "I suppose they will have to. But you know men. They get very stubborn when they feel they're being coerced into anything."

Moriah laughed. "Don't I ever."

"Are you gals bad-mouthing us guys again?" a male voice inquired. Kane appeared behind his wife. He wrapped his arms around her and proceeded to ravish her neck until she begged for mercy. A becoming flush highlighted her face when he finally lifted his head.

Carey smiled at their play, while ignoring a stab to her heart. She knew their story. They'd fallen in love as teenagers. It wasn't until Moriah had come back to find her father that Kane had discovered he was also a father. Moriah's teenage daughter had been his child. He and Moriah had fallen in love all over again. This time it had ended all right for them. They'd put the past behind and married.

"Time to get to work," Moriah said in a stern tone to her teasing husband. Her eyes were laughing, though.

Carey sighed after they left. She donned a colorful smock printed with fairy tale characters and went to greet her first patient.

She didn't see Wayne that day, or the next four. Neither did he call. Although she'd thought she was beyond false pride, she couldn't bring herself to call him.

The promised storm came through on Thursday night. On Friday, they awoke to a wonder world of white.

"The trees look like cupcakes," Sophie declared, her nose and Highway's pressed to the window. "All frosted with snow. Let's make cupcakes tonight, okay, Mom? When is Wayne coming over? Let's invite him to supper."

"He's very busy at the ranch. This snow will be hard on the cattle. The cowboys will have to feed them somehow."

"Oh." Sophie skipped to the table when Carey had their oatmeal and toast ready. Highway went to his dish and wolfed down the dog food she set out for him. His tail wagged when Sophie scolded him for eating so fast.

Carey had to wait until the snowplow came through and cleared her drive before she and Sophie could get on the road. When she returned home after dark that night, the snow was falling again. She and Sophie made cupcakes and decorated them with sprinkles. They played with the pup, had cupcakes with milk during a video, then read two books when Sophie was tucked into bed.

Carey, dressed in her warm flannel gown, sat in front of the fire and looked through the latest medical journal. The clock on the mantel chimed ten. She sighed as the loneliness washed over her and hugged her knees to her chest. She had to get a grip.

Her life had been fine before that drifter J. D. Cade had barged into it. He might be Wayne Kincaid in reality, but the golden boy who had once shown her a kindness bore no resemblance to the man who had come back from war. That man had been tempered by fire and come out as hard as stainless steel. It was all so sad.

Before she had time to get more than a little maudlin, she heard an engine on the drive. Going to the kitchen window, she peered into the night.

Snow came out of a vortex centered in the distant streetlight and hit the window with a faint crackling sound. Someone sat in a truck, looking her way, his headlights bright on the garage door.

She realized who it was. She gasped and her pulse increased. She opened the door to the garage and hit a button. The garage door rolled up. The pickup eased inside. The engine was turned off. Wayne swung out, slammed the door and strode toward her.

"Get inside. It's freezing out here."

He closed the door behind him, saw her bare feet, muttered something she didn't catch and swung her into his arms.

"What are you doing?" she demanded.

He grinned. "Not all I hope to do. Where did you lose your shoes?"

"At the sofa. I was reading—"

She got no further. He set her down on the cushions and proceeded to kiss her breathless. She shivered as the cold from his clothing surrounded her. He opened his jacket and pulled her inside, wrapping her in the warmth of sheepskin and his body. She sighed and savored it all.

"God, I've missed you," he muttered when they finally came up for air.

"You shouldn't be out. The weather is terrible." She touched him as she spoke, stroking his hair, his ears, his cheeks, which were warming slowly. "You could have had a wreck, gotten frostbite or—"

"Shh. None of those things happened. I'm here."

"Take your coat off. And your boots. I'll make you a warm drink."

"Okay if I take a hot shower?"

"Yes. Good idea." She fussed over him, helping him with his jacket, his boots and finally his clothing. "Are you hungry?"

"Yes."

Naked now, and in her bedroom, he grabbed her to him, stroking her through her gown, driving her mad with needs denied for the long, lonely week. He kissed her again, then set her away and headed for the shower.

She went to the kitchen and put out cupcakes on a plate, then made a thick sandwich of ham on rye and a pot of decaffeinated coffee. She considered, then set out two snifters and the brandy she kept for her father's visits. She took everything to the coffee table in the living room. There she sat and waited for him to come to her, while she weighed the past against the future.

She'd trusted her heart once before, and it had been wrong. Tomorrow he could be gone without a trace, just like the fog that crept down from the mountain into the valley at night, then disappeared come morning.

He returned wearing the pajamas she'd provided when he was recuperating from the surgery. Like Highway, he wolfed down the food as if he hadn't eaten all day. She poured them each a jot of brandy. He raised his glass in a silent toast.

She did the same.

They watched each other as they sipped the liquor. When she set the glass aside, he reached for her again.

"You feel good," he said, and kissed her.

"So do you. Did you get all the cattle moved before the storm?" she asked a full minute later.

His mouth kicked up at the corners. "Yes." He sighed and leaned his forehead against hers. "Today, all I could think about was you and being here."

"Oh."

She couldn't think of a word to add to that statement. Something warm and sweet and contented spread through her. It would be okay to tell him her dreams, then she would listen to his. Maybe they would be the same. Tomorrow, she would tell him.

But he was gone when she awoke.

Wayne pulled a blue crew-neck sweater on, adjusted the collar of his shirt, then added a wool sport jacket. The puppy tugged at his pant leg.

He scooped up the little rascal and put her in the box for the third time. "Stay," he ordered.

The pup tilted her head to one side as if considering, then hopped out again. Wayne caught her before she'd gone two feet. He closed the flaps on the box. She yapped in protest and kept it up until he let her out again.

"Just like a female," he groused at her.

She sat down, tilted her head to an alert angle and gave him a puppy-dog grin.

He ran a brush through his hair, which he'd had cut that afternoon. He'd been invited to the McCallums' for dinner. They were going to go over the ranch plans. He'd mentioned them briefly to Sterling the other day.

The deputy had seemed interested in his ideas for a possible ski resort and vacation spot along with a working ranch to attract visitors. There was enough land to run both operations. They could start small and expand slowly, maybe put in cross-country ski trails first.

Carey had mentioned several possibilities. She was a smart woman with a good head for business. That's one of the things he liked about her. She was capable and practical.

Thinking of her made him think of last night. He'd gone to her against his better judgment. He could feel himself being drawn in, the proverbial moth to candle, by her warmth and caring ways. And Sophie, too. She was a neat kid.

He frowned as feelings pushed against his insides, making him feel tight and uneasy.

All the plans they'd discussed for the combined Kincaid-Baxter spreads sounded pretty far-ranging. It would take a commitment of time and energy. She'd seemed to think he would be around to make all this happen. Had she forgotten he planned to leave when the problems were cleared up?

Hmm, Sterling had said Clint Calloway would be at dinner, too. It sounded as if the lawmen planned a big powwow. Maybe they had some news.

He picked up the rambunctious puppy, then headed out to the truck and drove to town. When he arrived at the deputy's home, he paused when he saw Carey's ute already there. He hadn't known she would be coming.

The internal pressure built a little more. For a moment, he thought of getting in the pickup and taking off, of hitting the road until he wound up as far from Whitehorn as he had when he'd been eighteen and had left. He could feel the tendrils of the Kincaid name reaching out to engulf him like morning glory winding around a post.

That's what happened if a man stayed in one place too long.

He tucked the pup in his inside jacket pocket and hurried up the sidewalk, his steps careful because the ground was covered in crusty snow that had melted, then frozen on top. He cursed once when he slipped and caught himself.

Sterling opened the door. "Come in. Sorry I didn't get the walk cleaned yesterday."

"That's okay. You lawmen types have more important things to do."

The deputy chief investigator grinned at his friendly gibe and held the door wide.

Wayne kept his arms folded over the front of his jacket, one hand inside to soothe the excitable pup. He'd cleared the gift with Jessica beforehand, having learned his lesson in dealing with mothers from Carey.

In the living room, he found Carey talking to Clint Calloway and his wife. He hesitated before stepping forward to shake hands with his half brother.

"This is my wife, Dakota," Clint said.

Wayne had once known her family. She'd been Dakota Winston of the Montana Winstons, an old family with mining, timber and cattle connections just like the Kincaids, and just as rich. Like him, she'd opted out of that life by becoming a cop. Interesting what people did to find a life of their own.

She had blue eyes that were a startling contrast to her black hair. For a cynical moment, he wondered if she was another of Jeremiah's bastard kids. She wasn't, but the more he learned of his father, the harder it was not to speculate about everyone he met.

"I didn't know you were going to be here tonight," he said to Carey. "Nice to see you."

Surprise darted through her eyes at his formality, but she smiled and asked him how he was feeling.

They each acted as if he hadn't spent the previous night in her bed. He'd left before first light to return to the ranch and the never-ending work there, but he'd been driven from her bed by more than a sense of duty.

"Fine. My hip hasn't bothered me at all. Tell Kane he did a good job." The squirming in his pocket reminded him he'd better not tarry over polite conversation. He glanced at Sterling. "I have a little something for Jennifer."

"She's in her room. Jessica is there with her. This way." He guided Wayne down the hall.

In the child's room, he found Sophie putting on a show with paper dolls for Jenny. The three-year-old, still thin, but not as pale, was laughing. The sound grabbed his heart and wouldn't let go.

"Hi, Wayne," Sophie cried, spotting him behind Sterling. "We're having a doll party. Want to come?"

His insides gave one of those painful twangs it was prone to lately at her cheerful welcome. "I have a little something for Jenny I thought she might like. You can give her some helpful hints on taking care of it."

Sophie's eyes widened. She erupted into giggles when he removed the puppy from his pocket. He set the little female on the bed beside Jenny. "It's a girl."

"She's mine?" Jenny looked at her mother. "Really mine? I can keep her?"

Jessica nodded. "You need to think of a name—oh."

At that moment, the pup squatted on the coverlet.

Wayne scooped it up and put it on the floor. "Sorry. I suggest she be kept in a box until she learns her manners."

Both girls stared at Jessica to see what she would say. The mother laughed and, grabbing a handful of tissues, swabbed up the drop on the cover and the rest on the floor.

"I think we can honestly say her new home has been duly christened." She looked at her husband. "Is there a box in the garage?"

After taking care of the minor emergency, the adults returned to the living room, leaving the girls to think of a name for the new pet.

"I hope it isn't a variety of Freeway," Carey mentioned drolly. She explained about Highway.

They came up with Byway, Pathway and Speedway as possibilities and were still laughing when they went in to dinner. Clint and Dakota sat on one side of the table, Wayne and Carey on the other.

She looked especially beautiful tonight. She wore a long plaid skirt of blue and brown and green with a thin black stripe. Her low-heeled boots were black. A sweater, green and clingy, showed off her figure—a fact that sent a warm hum through him. She'd even put on blush and a soft red lipstick. He smiled at that.

During the meal, he realized the others were already treating them as a couple. It added to his uneasiness. He was out of place in the family scene.

The chilly wind of forewarning slid down his neck. He'd need to leave soon. When spring came.

After they finished the meal, Jessica and Carey went to check on the girls, while Dakota volunteered to serve coffee. The three men settled in the living room.

Sterling cleared his throat. "I've been thinking."

Wayne tensed.

"Jessica and I want you two to share the ranch with Jennifer."

"Hey, no way. I don't want any part of the Kincaid holdings," Clint protested.

"Same here. I told you that," Wayne added. "The lawyer is drawing up a quit-claim now."

The deputy held up a hand as if stopping traffic. "Hear me out, please. If anything happened to me and Jessica, what would become of Jenny?"

The two men looked at each other, but neither had an answer.

"Exactly," Sterling said. "There'd be long-lost relatives coming out of the woodwork, wanting a piece of her inheritance. You two are the closest relatives she has. I know you both care about her. I want the Kincaid holdings split three ways among you."

"We're both grown men. We've made our lives," Wayne reminded the lawman. "Jenny has a future to look to."

"Maybe. If we can save the ranch. Luckily, it's paid for. The land and buildings are worth ten million. The cattle and machinery another million, maybe more. That's a lot for a kid to handle. I don't like the idea of Jenny having that hanging over her head."

Dakota brought in a tray with filled cups and carefully placed it on the coffee table. She glanced up sharply at this last announcement.

Clint shook his head. "Jeremiah Kincaid had nothing to do with me when he was alive. I don't want anything of his now that he's gone."

"I feel the same," Wayne said.

"That's not the point." Sterling gave each man a piercing stare, then settled on Wayne. "You're the only legitimate heir. Even when a case has been settled and after-discovered heirs discredited, it can be reopened on new evidence. If you died, someone could come forward as *your* heir and tie Jenny up in court for years...until the ranch is more than just strapped for cash. If it became flat broke, we'd have to sell out."

Wayne snorted. "You don't have to worry on my account. I don't have any heirs, legitimate or otherwise."

"But you might have a family someday," Sterling persisted. "They could grow to resent the fact that you gave up their heritage—"

"I don't intend to have any heirs, not now and not in the future." The words came out harsh, filled with the loathing he'd felt toward his father for his callous ways.

All the resentment of his youth boiled to the surface—the pressure to act as the Kincaid golden boy, the push on him to always be the best, the need to live up to someone else's standards and expectations.

He didn't want the baggage that came with being a Kincaid. He'd opted out of the life twenty-five years ago. There was no going back.

Jessica and Carey entered the room. From the way they avoided his eyes, he guessed they'd heard his declaration. Jessica took a seat next to her husband. Carey, instead of sitting beside him on the love seat, chose to perch on a chair across the room from him.

He cursed mentally, but didn't say anything to change or soften his choice of words.

Sterling took his wife's hand. "Jessica and I want to ask you two to be the legal guardians of Jenny in case something does happen to us. We'd like you to be co-owners with Jenny and trustees of the ranch along with us. We think that's best for all concerned." He glanced from one man to the other.

Clint rubbed a hand over his forehead. "I don't want anything from the Kincaid holdings, but I guess I could be a trustee, if you really think it's necessary." He looked at Dakota, who nodded and smiled approval at him.

Sterling answered. "I do."

Five pairs of eyes turned to Wayne.

He drew a deep breath. "I'll think about it. That's all I can promise."

"All right. At any rate, I'm having accounts set up for both of you and Jenny. Any profits the ranch makes will be equally divided among the three of you. Whether you ever claim it or not." His tone was final.

Jessica jumped to her feet. "We'll talk more another time. Now, let's have dessert. Carey brought over her famous sour cream pound cake with vanilla sauce."

The talk returned to the weather, which showed no

signs of a warming trend, and cattle prices, which were pretty good at the present. Sterling brought up the ranch again, his thoughts directed at Carey. They discussed the opening of her place and the Kincaid spread as a resort.

"We'd need someone to manage the whole operation, someone who had the big picture," Sterling said, looking at Wayne.

Wayne kept his thoughts to himself.

"Oh, I just remembered," Carey spoke up. "Moriah said her father wanted us to know that the outsiders aren't as pure as their name. Does that ring any bells—"

"Good God," Wayne muttered.

A scene from his past rushed into his mind—his father angry, Homer Gilmore watching from the bunkhouse porch where he'd stopped to cadge a dinner off the cook, himself seated beside the old codger. "PureGrow. That's who wanted the ranch years ago."

Clint leaned forward, his brow furrowed in thought. "PureGrow? That's the big agri-chemical company that was indicted for unapproved experiments on animals. If they're looking for land in a remote spot, you can bet it isn't for altruistic purposes."

"The charges were dropped," Sterling reminded him.

Clint's jaw set stubbornly. "They're bad news."

"Lester Buell was the link with PureGrow," Wayne said. "Have you had any further leads on the guy he called from his cell phone?"

Sterling looked at Clint. "Did Austin check out the rest of Widdermann's phone list yet?"

"He put in a request for his home and office calls.

We had to get a judge over in Missoula to okay it. Now that we have an idea what we're looking for, it should be easier."

Sterling relaxed. "Good. I want you to check Wendell Hargrove's phone lines, too."

"Wendell? He's the Kincaid estate attorney," Dakota murmured. "And a trustee along with you."

"Yeah." The chief investigator looked grim. "He's been pressing a little too hard to sell."

"I'll check it out," Dakota promised. She gave her husband a wry glance. "If my senior detective partner would like me to, that is."

"Okay, rookie," he drawled, "let's see if you've learned anything about law enforcement. What's the first thing you're going to do?"

"Put a secret tap on his line," she said in a dead-level voice.

Clint threw up his hands. "I taught her everything I know, and she still doesn't know anything."

That drew a laugh from the others.

"I'm going to Judge Walker and ask her pretty please to let us check on the attorney's calls," Dakota corrected.

"Good," Sterling said. "Clint, see if you can find any ties to PureGrow by anybody in town. I have some friends in the FBI who might be interested in their activities."

Wayne liked the way the deputy handled things. He was a thinking man. He glanced at Carey's closed expression. One thing about men, they didn't let emotion get in the way of sense. He was pretty sure she had stored up some quarrelsome words to share with him when they were alone....

Twelve

At nine, Carey indicated she needed to leave. Jenny had already fallen asleep, her hand on the box that contained the puppy. Sophie had watched a video while the adults talked, then she, too, went to sleep.

"I'll have to let you out," Wayne said. "I'm parked behind your ute."

"Thank you."

When she had the cranky Sophie ready, he lifted the child from her arms. "I'll carry her."

"Thanks." She pulled on her parka and followed Wayne to her ute after bidding a hasty good-night to the others. When she pulled onto the road, she wasn't surprised to see him follow at a safe distance behind her.

At her house, she entered the garage. He parked behind her on the driveway, then carried Sophie into the house for her. While she changed her daughter into pajamas, he waited in the living room. By the time she joined him, he had a fire going.

She paused at the door, watching him as he stared into the fire, a snifter of brandy in his hand. He sat on the sofa, his long legs stretched out and crossed at the ankles. He looked very much at home. And very restless in spite of his relaxed position.

He glanced up after a moment as if he sensed her observing him. "I helped myself. I hope you don't mind." He indicated the snifter of brandy.

"Of course not." She poured a tiny amount for herself and sat in the recliner-rocker.

"McCallum surprised me tonight with his ideas for splitting the ranch. Did you know about his plans?"

"No. Jessica and I hadn't discussed it, but I know they've been worried about the Kincaid place and Jenny's future. Were you aware Lexine Baxter kidnapped Jenny when it came out that the child belonged to Jeremiah and everyone assumed she would inherit the ranch along with Dugin Kincaid? I think they're afraid for Jenny."

"They think there's safety in numbers?" he questioned, his gaze on the fire.

"They also think it's unfair that all of Jeremiah's children don't share equally in their heritage, no matter how you feel about your father personally."

"And you? What do you think?"

"I agree with them."

"I thought you might."

She met his gaze levelly. "What does that mean?"

His smile was cynical. "You admitted you once had a crush on me, on who I was once. Are you seeing the Kincaid name in your future?"

She considered carefully before she spoke. "I thought there might be a future for *us*. It had nothing to do with your name, whether Cade, Kincaid or Smith or Brown or Jones. I thought you might want to stay."

He stood abruptly and paced the narrow space in front of the fireplace before propping his foot on the hearth and staring pensively into the flames again.

Carey steeled herself for what was to come. She was suddenly glad she hadn't changed into her nightgown. It seemed important that she be dressed and formal with him while he told her he was leaving.

"So when are you going?" she finally asked.

"As soon as we know the truth about the ranch."

"I see."

He drank the last swallow of brandy and placed the glass on the mantel. He looked at her then. "I tried to be honest about us and the future."

"You're going to walk away from here, from White-horn and people who care for you. Why? What life beckons you to another place? Sterling would like you to manage the ranch as a resort. With Rand Harding staying on as foreman, you could oversee the entire operation—"

"I don't want the ties," he said.

"Ah, yes." She clamped her lips shut before she said something she might regret. If love could hold a person, he would stay, because she and Sophie loved him.

"I didn't mean to hurt you," he said in a low voice.

She glanced at him, then shrugged. "I learned long ago that people must choose their own course. You have to love enough to give up that elusive thing called freedom for the comfort and yes, the ties, of home."

His eyes darkened at her answer. "I...care about you and Sophie."

"We love you. There's the difference." She met his gaze. "We want you to stay and build a life here with us. We need you."

He shook his head. "You're a doctor, a wonder woman who can do anything you set your mind to. Sophie is a happy soul. It was Freeway she fell in love with. Now she has Highway. She'll never miss me."

"Is that how you ease your conscience when you leave a place? You tell yourself that no one will miss you?" She stood and crossed her arms, hugging the growing misery inside. "I'll miss you. I want you to want me so much you can't bear to leave. Sophie wants a brother or sister. I'd like to give her one. I'd like it to be our child, Wayne. Yours and mine. That's my dream. What is yours?"

"I gave up on dreams a long time ago." He growled the words, an angry flush creeping into his cheeks.

"Too bad. Sometimes they're all that make life bearable." She went to the front door and flipped on the outside lights. "Please go now. I don't see any sense in discussing this further."

He grabbed up his jacket and hat. He paused in front of her. "I told you I was leaving."

"Yes. You were never less than open and above-board in your intentions." She managed a smile. "It's just that I always have this need to save people, even from themselves."

She forced herself to stillness when he let his fingers drift across her cheek. "You're one hell of a woman, Carey Hall."

"If you say I'll make some man a wonderful wife, I'll stick you with the biggest hypodermic I can find," she warned. She opened the door.

The frigid March air blasted inside, producing shivers as she waited for him to leave.

He bent and pressed a light kiss on her mouth, then he jammed his hat on and walked out into the night.

Carey dashed toward the Hip Hop Café, her steps uneven as she dodged puddles on the sidewalk. She was starved. She hadn't had time for lunch as the morning patients spilled over into the afternoon. It was almost nine now.

Lorrie had called and let her say good-night to Sophie before putting the child to bed. Carey had finished at the office, then headed for the hospital for evening rounds.

Somehow her plan of keeping shorter hours didn't seem to be working. She'd had an influx of cases lately. Three car wrecks that week.

She'd assisted Kane in surgery on two children who had been seriously injured in one of the accidents. One child hadn't been wearing a seat belt. That made her want to commit havoc on the parent.

"Carey, honey, come join us," a female voice called out when she entered the café.

She wiped the cold drizzle from her face and glanced around. Lily Mae Wheeler waved her toward a chair. Winona Cobb, the local psychic, was with Lily Mae. Now *there* was a study in contrasts.

Lily Mae wore a knitted outfit of dark green with big squares of fake jewels sewn on the material. Her earrings brushed her shoulders. Her hair was a strawberry blond at present, but that could change at any time. Her makeup was extravagant, to say the least.

Winona was a short, plump woman in a long brown-and-gray dress of sixties vintage. Her gray hair was pulled into a crown of braids on her head. She wore small turquoise earrings and no makeup at all on her weathered face. A collection of amulets and crystals on thin silken cords hung from around her neck.

Carey joined them. "Hello. I've been praying for spring, but I don't remember asking that it rain every day of the season. Winona, are you getting any vibes?"

"Only in my arthritis," the older woman said with a twinkle in her eyes.

Carey ordered the special when the waitress came.

Janie lingered after taking the order. "It was sure a surprise about Wayne Kincaid, wasn't it?"

"Umm, yes, it was," Carey replied in a professional tone, her smile cool. She ignored the squeezing sensation in her chest at the mention of his name. She hadn't seen Wayne in two weeks, but she knew he was still at the ranch.

Jessica had reported the three men—Sterling, Wayne and Clint—were very involved with plans for the ranch. She had noticed that she wasn't included, so the skiing idea must have been dropped.

"You didn't know that J. D. Cade was really the long-lost heir?"

"No, I didn't," Carey said with complete honesty. "It was as much of a surprise to me as everyone."

When she didn't say anything else, Janie ambled off toward the kitchen to turn in her order. However, her appetite had fled. She wished she'd gone home and heated leftovers instead of stopping here.

"I'm hearing good reports on little Jennifer McCallum," Lily Mae said, her expression openly disappointed when Carey didn't add anything about the elusive Wayne Kincaid.

"She's doing fine." This time Carey's smile was genuine. "Would you believe she's gained five pounds since the transplant? Dr. Hunter and I are delighted, of course. This was a first for Whitehorn and proves such treatment can be performed at small, regional hospitals as well as the large teaching ones."

Lily Mae's eyes glazed over long before Carey finished expounding on the benefits of hometown medicine as opposed to big-city treatments. Winona's smile widened fractionally.

It didn't take long for Lily Mae to find another topic for her inveterate curiosity about people. "My, there's Sam Brightwater and that girl who came here looking for her father. I was sure surprised when he up and married an outsider like that."

"Julia Stedman," Winona said. "The marriage will be good for both of them."

Carey didn't report that Julia had nearly lost the child she carried. Sam's child. He'd hovered over her at the hospital, his eyes filled with loving concern—

Tears burned her eyes, shocking her at how close her emotions were to the surface. She took a calming breath and let it out slowly and steadily.

Life went on. That was another thing she'd learned in medical practice. Death strolled by and selected its targets at will, it sometimes seemed, but life continued for those who were left behind.

And sometimes a life was wrestled out of the grip of Death and he was sent away empty-handed. Like Jenny. Like Sam and Julia's coming baby.

The door opened and a momentary lull engulfed the small crowd of late diners at the restaurant. She glanced over her shoulder. Wayne Kincaid was at the door, shaking water off his jacket and hanging it up.

He didn't look around, but headed straight for the counter, where he dropped his lanky frame onto a stool and ordered the special when Janie came over. He looked tired.

A professional assessment, Carey assured herself.

Winona reached over and took her hand. Carey looked a question at the older woman. Winona shook her head, then closed her eyes.

"Oh," Lily Mae said.

Carey put a finger to her lips.

"It won't always be like this," Winona said in a quiet

tone. "I see…I see…something in your future, your heart's desire . . . a Christmas gift…."

Carey's smile turned cynical. She tried to think of a present she might want. She couldn't, certainly not anything she would consider her heart's desire. Besides, Christmas was nine months away.

Nine months.

She swallowed and held very still, while Winona frowned and shook her head as if unable to see more. Carey, although a scientist from a medical point of view, didn't discount other, more spiritual, qualities in healing. She'd seen cases turn around for no reason that science could detect.

Besides, Winona had been a staple of Whitehorn society too long for Carey to ignore her predictions.

Winona sighed and opened her eyes.

The two women gazed at each other as knowledge of love and hope and dreams long discarded flashed between them. The sensation was as elemental as fire and water, earth and air.

The strange moment passed. Winona removed her hand. Janie served the dinner special. Carey picked up her fork.

Across the way, she found Wayne looking at her through an old-fashioned wall mirror with antlers attached to it for a hat rack. Her gaze locked with his, but it was like looking at opaque blue granite. There was no sense of depth or shared feelings between them.

She looked back at her plate and began eating. Lily Mae and Winona waited until she finished, then they all left together, walking out into the night and the storm.

When Carey was safely buckled into her sports utility vehicle, she sat there for a minute, but no rangy figure emerged from the café to seek her out.

Realizing she was waiting for him, she turned the key and headed for home. She had her child and her career. Once they had been enough. They would be again.

Sterling made a face at the bitter coffee in his cup. "I can't figure out why Jessica's coffee always turns out good, while mine turns out awful, even using the same pot."

Wayne smiled briefly at the gripe. He held the quit-claim agreement in his hand. Sterling had refused to accept it, had even made threatening remarks such as going to Kate and getting Jeremiah's will reopened.

"You look as if you've been marooned on a desert island with nothing but my coffee to drink for a month."

"Yeah, well, spring on a ranch keeps a man hopping. Harding hasn't been able to get us more help. Cowboys don't want to hire on because of the Kincaid curse."

"Yeah, they're a bunch of cowards," Sterling said cheerfully. With his daughter rapidly improving, the lawman was feeling good these days.

Wayne snorted in disgust. He would be lucky to leave by fall at the rate things were going toward solving the mystery at the ranch. "Haven't you found out anything at all?" he demanded.

"We've been checking—"

A knock sounded on the door.

"Ah, this may be what we've been looking for. Come in," he called.

Clint Calloway and Reed Austin entered. They were both smiling. Reed plunked a couple of papers down on the desk.

"It's there. We got the connection," Reed told them with the cheeky triumph of a policeman who finally has a case going his way.

"And the man," Clint added, his eyes narrowing to dangerous slits. "We arrested Widdermann on the old Baxter property this morning. He was spreading those poisoned mineral blocks again."

"Good," Sterling said approvingly, his eyes on the list of calls. "Damn," he said.

Wayne tensed, waiting for the news.

"It's Hargrove. He's the one working with Pure-Grow." Sterling glanced up at Wayne. "I had a trace put on his calls, too. He's the middleman, not Lester Buell. Lester knows he's a front for PureGrow, but I'll bet he doesn't know about Wendell. There doesn't seem to be a connection between them. Wendell has covered his tracks well."

"Do we need a tap on his phone?" Clint asked.

"Yes. Call Judge Walker. She knows the case. This private line into his home office is the one he used with PureGrow. That's the one we want to watch."

After the two younger officers left, Sterling rubbed his chin thoughtfully and stared at Wayne.

"Yeah?" Wayne felt compelled to ask. Whatever was

on the deputy's mind, he'd listen, but he wasn't going to be talked into anything.

"Are you still set on leaving?" Sterling asked.

He nodded.

"Isn't this carrying defiance of your dad to extremes?"

Wayne reared back from the unexpected attack. "What the hell does that mean?"

"You tell me."

"I have no idea what you're getting at. Why don't you put it in plain English?"

Sterling nodded. He leaned forward and crossed his arms on the battered desk. "You could have a lot going for you here."

"Such as?"

"A heritage that has a long history in this county." Sterling's voice dropped to a lower tone. "A fine woman and a great kid who love you. You could have a home with them—"

"I don't need a home. Freeway and I have gotten along just fine on our own for years. I mean to keep it that way."

"No emotional bonds, huh?" Sterling nodded wisely. "Yeah, it's better that way. Takes guts to risk having your heart yanked out by the roots by the person you love."

Wayne clenched his hands and tried to block out images of Carey. It was no use. He saw her in all the settings she moved between, sparkling like a fine jewel whether at the hospital or office, her home, the cabin or the funny little café with its offbeat decor.

Sterling plied him with a piercing gaze. "I think we

have this case all but wrapped up. Can you stay on at the ranch another month?"

"I suppose."

"When word gets out about PureGrow being behind the Kincaid troubles, we should be able to hire back our old hands with no trouble. You'd be free to leave then."

"Fine."

Sterling heaved a deep breath, as if preparing to take the bull by the horns. "Jessica and I have some money saved up. We'd like to invest it in the resort. I'm thinking of maybe me, you, Clint and the doc going in together as partners in a corporation, the Beartooth Resort."

"The doc? Carey?"

"Yeah. As you pointed out, she's got the land with the natural ski slopes on it, plus the old mining town. We could lease the land from the two ranches. Clint and I are pretty well committed to it. So is his wife. I believe she'll bring some of the Winston money in. Your part of the deal is managing the operation."

Wayne stood as a wave of restlessness rushed through him. "Sounds as if you have it all figured out."

"Are you in?" the lawman asked, putting the future on the line. "If you walk, the offer won't be repeated."

The shrewd grin of the other man put Wayne on the spot. He was being told to make a decision. And when he did, one way or the other, his fate would be sealed.

"I'll get back to you."

Sterling nodded, his manner noncommittal, but his gaze assessing. Wayne figured he came up short in the lawman's eyes. But what he was asking—for him to come back and take on the Kincaid persona again—that wasn't an easy thing.

Twenty-five years of freedom down the tubes. Twenty-five years of being free of Jeremiah Kincaid.

Of course, the old man was dead, so that wasn't the problem anymore, but still, he'd grown used to being on his own, doing his own thing....

Until he knew whether he could give up his roaming life and settle down, he wasn't going to commit himself to anyone or anything. It wouldn't be right.

He walked out of the courthouse feeling more than a little hounded. Like a cornered elk, he had a feeling he should have started running months ago.

Carey looked out the windows. The rain had stopped and the sun had dried up the puddles. It looked as if spring might be truly there. The air still had a nip, but buttercups were pushing up blooms beside her drive. The neighbor's tulips were starting to open.

She and Sophie had visited her folks over Easter; now Sophie was spending spring break with her father and his new live-in girlfriend. It looked serious between the couple. Carey wished them well.

The total lack of rancor in her heart toward her ex-husband had both surprised and pleased her. Odd, but now he seemed to be someone she had once known, a classmate maybe, not someone she had loved.

Life goes on.

She smiled at the homily, then sighed. She'd had a light day at the office. With no patients in the hospital at present, she was free in the evenings, too. Time clicked by at a slow pace.

On an impulse, she changed to jeans, packed a sandwich for dinner and headed out to the cabin. She would measure the place where she wanted to add some shelves. Maybe she should think of adding a bedroom to make it more comfortable for weekend visiting.

She arrived at the cabin at five. In thirty minutes, she was finished with her measurements and sketches of the interior. She'd decided to see about putting in a well and a pump so she'd have running water inside. Maybe she should build a whole new house.

Shaking her head ruefully at how quickly she'd gone from simple shelves to a major construction project, she drifted outside. She walked across the small clearing and strolled toward the trail through the woods.

One of her favorite spots was the ridge of cap rock that separated this part of the old Baxter holdings from the Kincaid ranch. From the ridge, she would be able to see most of the Kincaid spread on one side and all the way to the Crazy Mountains on another. She studied the clouds that had gathered over the tallest peaks. It might rain.

Then again, it might not. She'd hike to the ridge and eat her supper, then head back before it got dark.

She stopped by the ute and strapped her fanny pack in place, checked the flashlight she carried, grabbed a jacket, then started off. Thirty minutes later, she arrived at the rugged limestone outcropping that sliced the two ranches with an almost straight line of rock that ended in a fairly impressive cliff.

At the bluff, sitting on one of the weathered stones, she let her legs dangle over the side while she observed the cattle in the fields and on the slopes of the gentler hills surrounding the pasture.

Sterling had called to offer her the going market value for grazing rights and had insisted she take the money. He was a fair-minded person, a little stiff and stern, but very likable. She thought Jessica had made a big difference in his life.

As she sat there musing and gazing into space, she nearly missed the truck coming along the dirt road from the Kincaid place. When she did notice it, her heart gave a giant leap, then beat very hard. It was Wayne's pickup.

Acting on the theory that it was hard to spot someone who didn't move, she sat still while he drove up to the corner of the fence line. He stopped and climbed down from the truck without glancing up at the ridge. She hardly let herself breathe.

He checked the tightness of the wire, then tossed a big mineral block into each of the fields on either side of the rutted road. She watched him do a fast head count on the cattle. She recalled her dad telling how Jeremiah Kincaid could come within ten cows of the correct number of mother-and-baby pairs in a field with just a glance.

Wayne counted the same way she did—by estimating blocks of ten. He checked the numbers on both sides of the road, then leaned against the truck fender and watched the animals mill around the mineral lick.

She huffed impatiently when he crossed his arms over his chest and looked as if he might take root on the spot.

Until he left, she was trapped up there. Unless she decided she didn't care if he saw her. And really, why should she mind? She was on her own land.

Her breath hung in her throat when he pushed away from the pickup and started up the trail that wound to the top of the cap rock. She muttered a word that would have earned her a mouth washing in her younger days.

As soon as he was out of sight where the trail ambled behind that copse of trees, she would take off and be out of there before he reached the point where the trails merged.

She tensed, then sprang into action as soon as he was no longer in view. She ran for the upper trail, her heart going lickety-split. She had to get past that first section of trees. Almost there. Almost…

He stepped onto the trail.

Carey almost ran him over.

A strong arm caught her as she skidded to a halt. "Going somewhere?" he asked.

"To the cabin," she said, panting.

He didn't appear to be breathing hard, but he had to have run to make it up the trail so fast.

"You saw me," she accused, angry that he'd been so sneaky about it. "You knew I was here."

"Yeah. Were you going to run home without saying hello?" he asked laconically, letting her go when she stepped back.

"Yes."

His smile belied the tension she sensed in him. She watched him warily.

"How have you been?" he asked.

Thirteen

"Fine." Carey, short of making a fool of herself and insisting on being allowed to pass, was trapped on the narrow trail with him. She took in his lean, masculine appearance.

He was wearing jeans and scuffed boots, a blue shirt that couldn't match his eyes for color and a black down vest. He pushed his hat up off his forehead, his gaze never leaving hers.

Lifting her chin, she held her ground and waited for his next move.

"Where's Sophie?"

"At her father's."

"How's Highway?"

"Fine." She shifted restlessly. "I have to be going." She took a step forward.

He moved aside, but when she was abreast of him, he held out a hand in front of her. A fat raindrop landed in his palm. "It's starting to rain."

She examined the clouds that were fast descending over the land. A sheet of rain was visible coming at them.

He grabbed her arm. "Come on, let's get to the truck."

She ran with him down the trail, and they reached the truck before the deluge hit.

"That was close," he said, laughing as the drops pounded the windshield.

She frowned at the heavy curtain of rain. She would have to ask him for a ride to the cabin. She wished she hadn't come out at all. It had been stupid.

"Would you mind giving me a lift to the cabin? My truck is there."

"Are you spending the night?"

She shook her head. "I have an early day tomorrow."

"Umm," he said as if he could see through her lie. However, he didn't probe further.

Neither spoke as he drove up the rough cattle road and over the ridge. When he pulled into the clearing, she already had her hand on the door handle.

"Wait," he requested.

The silence between them could have been a snow chasm a mile deep. Neither was willing to make the leap across.

"Yes?" she finally said impatiently.

"The case was solved today. Did you hear?"

"No."

"Wendell Hargrove was arrested. Because the crimes went across state lines, the FBI was brought in. Five indictments to commit conspiracy, fraud and extortion, unlawful entry and destruction of property at peril to life were laid against three officers of PureGrow and the attorney."

"Well." Her hand crept toward the door handle. "That's wonderful. Now the ranch can get back to functioning. And you can leave," she added, keeping her tone bright.

"Hell," he murmured.

He tossed his hat onto the gun rack and slid close. His arms encircled her. Her breath came fitfully between her lips as he bent to her. His mouth touched hers lightly.

"Please don't," she whispered. The misery of the past week without Sophie to distract her rushed over her.

"One for the road," he bargained, tilting his head to one side to study her averted face.

She shook her head.

"I'm leaving at the end of the month," he said, as if that argument might sway her. "Eleven days."

"You're not going to help Sterling with the ranch or the resort if they get it started?"

"You can't imagine a person leaving when someone else might need him, can you?" He caught a handful of her hair and let it slide through his fingers. "Quitting isn't in your vocabulary."

There was amusement and exasperation in his voice,

and other emotions she couldn't identify. His perusal was one of dazzling tenderness. It hurt and confused and angered her. The tears she'd suppressed for days welled close to the surface. She breathed slowly and deeply.

"I haven't said this to a woman in twenty-five years, but I think I'm in love with you."

Rage flew through her. He said he was leaving and in the next breath said he was in love? What kind of logic was that?

She batted his hand away from her cheek. Tears poured down her face as hard as the rain pounded the pickup. "See what you've done? You've made me cry."

With that, she had the door open and was out of there.

He was still sitting in the same place when she pulled out of the clearing in front of the cabin with a spinning of tires on the wet dirt.

Wayne tossed the last shirt into the bag, then looked around the room he'd called home for a year. Yeah, he had everything. He zipped the carryall, then hefted it to his shoulder. He picked up the already full duffel. That was it, down to the travel alarm he'd carried for years but never used. He was ready to move out.

Not a soul was on hand to witness his departure when he went outside. He tossed the bags into the truck and paused for one last glance around the place.

Harding and the cowboys, including the new hands they'd hired on now that the Kincaid curse had been resolved, were moving cattle to the high pastures for summer.

He'd always liked that part of ranching best—the spring and the ambling up into the hills, camping out along the swollen creeks, sleeping in the truck or the snow cabins along the way, observing what winter had done to the land.

A twang echoed through his chest as if a single note on a harp had been strummed.

Turning from the hills, he looked over the home pastures. The mares lazed in the sun while their foals raced one another along the fence. Freeway lay in the grass by the barn, his two remaining pups tumbling over him while they wrestled with each other and tried to entice the old man into playing with them. He frowned as another twang hit him in the chest.

He let his gaze drift over the stables, barns and sheds until he came to the ranch house. He stared at it for a long spell as scenes from the past rushed into his mind.

Overbuilt and ostentatious, nevertheless it had been his home for the first eighteen years of his life. He'd learned about life there, its cruelties, its sly jokes on naive humans....

Its joys?

Yeah, there had been those.

Enough of memories. It was time to go. He'd said his farewells to Jenny and Clint and the McCallums yesterday. He'd promised to write and visit often.

"Yo, Freeway, get your mangy hide in the truck, fellow. The road is calling." He glanced over at the big mutt.

Freeway thumped his tail briefly, then laid his head between his paws and yawned.

Wayne hauled the door open and waved his hat toward the interior. "Last call," he said. "Either you're with me or you're on your own."

Freeway got to his feet, stretched with his rump in the air and his head between his forefeet, then trotted over and jumped into the truck. He took his place on the passenger side. His pups tried to follow.

"Sorry, guys, but you have to stay here. Your mom would worry if she came back from driving cattle and found you gone. You'll be okay."

He put the pups in the stable, closed the door and jumped in the pickup. Thirty minutes later, he slowed down as he entered the city limits of Whitehorn.

For a couple of blocks, he kept his thoughts grimly centered on getting to the highway and heading south. Then at Center Street, he turned and drove slowly through the heart of the town, past the Hip Hop Café, the park, the courthouse and sheriff's department.

Finally he turned toward the west and drove to the cemetery, knowing he had to do this one last thing before he left. He parked and climbed down, leaving the door open in case Freeway wanted to join him. He walked along the rows until he came to the Kincaid section.

There he stopped and read the headstones. His father. His mother. His brother. All laid to rest in neatly divided rectangles. Too bad life wasn't as orderly as death.

The twang hit his chest again, harder this time.

He stepped inside the wrought-iron picket fence and sat on a stone bench at the foot of his mother's grave. Taking off his hat, he contemplated the lives of the three people who'd made up his family.

Dugin had been neither a scholar nor an athlete. He'd stayed on at the ranch, but he'd never found his niche in life. His mother, gentle and loving, but stubborn…or maybe it was pride that wouldn't let her admit she'd made a mistake in marrying Jeremiah or that the marriage was over long before she passed on.

And Jeremiah. Smart, capable, a man who thought he owned life…and the lives of all those around him. He'd died an ignoble death in his own bathtub, done in by Lexine Baxter, who'd been harder and craftier than anyone Jeremiah had ever known. The old man had met his match in Dugin's scheming wife.

And then there had been himself. The golden boy. The quarterback with the deadly arm. The A student. The "pick of the litter," his dad had once called him, chest puffed out as he took his son's accomplishments for his own.

That boy was gone, too.

Wayne was surprised to realize it no longer hurt, none of it, the betrayals, the memories, the roughshod manner of his father. He saw that young, idealistic young man as a separate being from himself and what he was now. He looked back into the past and saw the golden boy as if he'd been another kid brother, one who'd died before his prime as poor Dugin had.

So it all came down to the same in the end. No matter

how many monuments a person built for himself in life, it all came down to six feet of dirt under a pretty lawn.

The Kincaid name wasn't much in these parts anymore. It was best to let it die out naturally—a family gone to seed and scattered in the wind.

The breeze ruffled his hair, reminding him it was time to be moving on. He jammed his hat on and turned his face from the tombs and the life he'd left behind long ago.

Freeway was gone when he reached the truck. He whistled, then waited, his elbow propped on the open window frame, the sun warm on his face as he surveyed the snow-dappled mountains. He whistled again.

"Freeway," he yelled, impatient to be off.

From a distance, he heard a faint bark. Peering down the road, he spied the dog loping off in the distance.

Muttering an imprecation, he drove down the country road until he caught up with the mutt. He stopped and reached across the front seat to open the passenger door.

"You weird dog, what the hell are you doing?"

Freeway dropped his tail and cringed, but didn't leap into the seat. He headed down the road at a faster clip. After a few yards, he looked back, barked once, then headed off again.

Wayne watched him for a couple of minutes, then closed the door, eased into gear and followed a few yards behind the mongrel, who seemed to have a destination in mind.

Within another half mile, Wayne knew where it was.

He cursed roundly, then gunned the engine. He was parked in the drive when Freeway came bounding across the lawn, barking joyfully as if he were Lassie and had just made it home.

The mutt dashed past Wayne and—

"Hey, hello, there," Carey said, laughing and avoiding the tongue that was trying to give her doggie kisses all over her face as Freeway propped his front paws on her chest and greeted her.

She'd stopped at the corner of the garage, her back partially to him as she patted Freeway and fended off the exuberant greeting at the same time. She hadn't seen him.

Wayne felt as if he'd been carved from stone. He couldn't move. He hadn't meant to see her again.

The twangs strummed painfully with each beat of his heart, and blood rushed to his head, making him dizzy. A whole ball of mixed emotions churned in his throat.

At that moment, Carey stepped back and looked his way. Wariness skittered into her eyes. Freeway dropped to the driveway and danced all around her as she came forward.

"Hello," she said, a question in the word. She looked at Freeway, then at him. "What's happening?"

"Freeway wanted to stop and say goodbye."

"Oh."

Her bouncy curls caressed her neck and forehead as the breeze shifted to the west. She was dressed in her old faded-green sweats, a gardening trowel in her hand. She wore one glove. She probably thought the other one was lost, but he could see it sticking out of her back pocket, where she'd tucked it for safekeeping.

A smile kicked up the corners of his mouth.

Her eyes widened in surprise, but she smiled back. "Well, have a nice trip. Have you decided where you're going this time?"

He shook his head. "Where're Sophie and Highway?"

"He's snoozing in the house. He wore himself out chasing bees and butterflies in the garden. Sophie's with her grandparents this weekend, attending her father's wedding. She'll be back tomorrow night. I'll tell her you stopped."

He nodded.

A flicker of uncertainty flashed through her eyes as he continued to stand there. He couldn't seem to tear his gaze from her. Or force his feet to move.

"Jennifer is doing well," she finally said. She removed the glove and dropped it and the trowel beside a flat of mixed annuals she was planting beside the garage. "She's gaining weight. Her hair is growing back."

"That's good." His voice came out husky and low, filled with tension that was growing with each second.

The wind toyed with her hair and pressed her clothing against her body, outlining the curves he knew. A shot of anticipated pleasure sped through him, stirring him to instant arousal.

"I hope you'll keep in touch. With the McCallums," she added hastily. A flush crept into her cheeks.

Something tender nudged his heart. The twangy

feeling made breathing difficult. Freeway went to the kitchen door and barked, demanding entrance. From inside, a series of excited yelps answered.

"I suppose we'd better let father and son say their farewells." She led the way toward the house.

Wayne followed, calling himself all kinds of names for not hightailing it out of there while he could. He shook his head. Okay, maybe he'd have a cup of Carey's great coffee, then he'd hit the road. For sure.

They went inside.

Highway jumped all over them, welcoming each entry into the kitchen as if each were a long-lost love. He and Freeway got into a game of tug-of-war with a rawhide chew.

"Coffee?"

"Umm, yes." He inhaled deeply. "Something smells good."

"I'm trying a new recipe for gingerbread. Sophie and I are going to make a gingerbread house for the class party at the end of school. Would you like some?"

He thought about it for about two seconds. "Sure."

"I'll make the sauce."

She poured the coffee, then made a vanilla-and-raisin sauce for the gingerbread. In a few minutes, she placed a plate in front of him and one for herself on the table.

"Be careful. The sauce is hot." She took the chair opposite. She checked the sauce by carefully sticking her tongue to a dab on her fork. "It's okay." She took a bite.

It was the best gingerbread he'd eaten in years. Maybe ever. In fact, he couldn't remember when he'd last had the treat. While chewing the second bite, an odd thing happened.

The past slipped from his mind.

He looked at Carey and everything left his mind, except for her…and him…and the growly sounds the dogs were making as they played…and the sound of the wind roaming around the eaves…and the sound of the clock ticking quietly on a shelf.

"You're beautiful," he said.

Her eyelashes flicked upward. He gazed into those blue-brown-golden depths, willing her to hold his glance.

"Thanks." She looked down and went on eating.

He drew a slow breath. The twangs quieted a bit, becoming calmer as he acknowledged and accepted the inevitable. "There's no way I can leave," he told her. "I'd have to tear my heart out by the roots, because it's going to stay right here in Whitehorn."

Her mouth dropped open, but she didn't speak.

"With you and Sophie."

She licked her lips and pressed them firmly closed.

He frowned. "Say something. I feel like a fool left hanging out in the wind to dry."

"I don't know what to say."

"Try 'I love you' for starters."

She shook her head and stared at him as if he'd gone completely crazy. Maybe he had. Or maybe he'd come to his senses. About damned time.

"Okay. How about 'Yes, Wayne, I'll marry you, even though you're ornerier and meaner and uglier than that mangy mutt you hang out with?' Can you say that?"

"No."

"Hmm, you're going to make me sweat it, huh? Okay, I'll go first." He cleared his throat, then stood. He paced to the counter and turned. "I thought I could walk away from here. I thought I could get in my truck and drive out of Whitehorn and not look back."

She bit into her bottom lip and looked as if she might cry. He wondered how many times she'd wept after she left him that day at her cabin. Regret strummed across his heartstrings.

"I couldn't." He paused, seeing the three graves lined up in a neat row. They were gone—his dad and mom and brother—but he was here and alive. "I went to the cemetery, instead, and said goodbye to the past."

Desperation washed over him as the full impact of all the things he wanted rushed at him in a tidal wave of need and longing.

"I love you. If you can bring yourself to believe that for now, I'll spend the rest of my life proving it to you. I'm through running, Carey, from myself and from you."

She stood, her expression wary, and yet, he thought he saw a glimmer in her eyes. "For how long?"

"Forever. If you'll have me, I'd like to stay here and build a life. I'd like to have that child you spoke of, that brother or sister for Sophie. Maybe one of each."

Carey felt as if her heart had grown too big for her chest. She pressed a hand against the ache and tried to understand what he was saying. She heard the words, but they were so foreign to what she'd expected, they could have been another language.

"I'm not sure I can believe you," she said.

"I know it's hard. But you're brave…." His persuasive smile turned up the corners of his mouth. "For a woman. Don't disappoint me now."

She gave him an indignant glare. He laughed, then opened his arms. She stayed where she was. He crowded in, pressing her, urging her with his rough velvet voice.

"Come on, Carey. Don't be a coward," he murmured. "I've confessed all. Tell me you'll marry me and save me from a lonely old bachelor's life."

"It's what you deserve."

"I know."

There was laughter in the words, but his eyes were serious. She gazed up at that incredible blue force and he had her. She couldn't look away. All the reasons she should reject him fled her mind.

"I want to believe," she heard herself confess.

"Do," he urged. He nuzzled her temple. His lips were soft, so soft and beguiling. His body was warm, snuggling up to hers, fitting them together just so….

She realized what was happening. "Wait. I need to think—"

"I love a thinking woman," he said. His hands cupped her behind while he brushed slowly from side to side. Riptides of longing crashed through her.

"A year," she said desperately, hanging on to reason by a thin thread. "If you stay here a year, then I'll consider marriage—"

"I've already been here a year."

"Oh."

She caught his hands and stopped their roaming ways. He let her guide them away from her hips, then he took over. He brought their hands behind her back and captured both wrists in one grip. Then he slipped his free hand under her top.

"Just as I suspected," he said, cupping her breast. "Outside and not wearing a bra. What would your neighbors think?"

"How would they know?" she demanded, trying to free her hands and move away. It was impossible.

"I might tell them if you don't do exactly what I tell you for the next…mmm, fifty years or so."

"Wayne—"

"Yes, love?" He kissed the side of her neck.

She squirmed as he deliberately skimmed over her tickle spot. His hand rubbed back and forth on her breast. Her nipple contracted into a tight bud. The heat built in her. Her resistance was melting into a pool of golden butter. Languor crept over her, warm and smooth and sensuous.

"Are you sure?" she asked.

He lifted his head and looked deep into her eyes. "Absolutely." He tilted his head toward Freeway. "Ask him. He knew I couldn't leave."

As if he knew exactly what was being said, Freeway looked at them and barked twice, his tail going like a banner in the wind. Highway couldn't resist. He launched himself at his old man. They tumbled over the floor in cheerful abandon.

Carey sighed. "All right."

Wayne gave her a cocky grin. "You won't be sorry."

"Huh. I'll let you know about that. In fifty years or so."

He laughed, then in a sudden move tossed her over his shoulder. When she shrieked like a banshee, he patted her on the backside. "I love a noisy woman."

In the bedroom, her laughter faded. He, too, went serious as they helped each other undress. When she would have clambered on the bed, he caught her hand. Lifting her into his arms, he placed her on the sheet, then ran his hand down the length of her body from her neck to her ankle.

"I never thought I would feel this way again about a woman," he murmured, watching her with great tenderness in his eyes. His gaze locked with hers. "You make me feel young."

"The golden boy," she said, smiling. She lightly touched the scars that laced his thigh.

He shook his head. "Not him. That boy is gone."

Carey's heart ached for all the pain he'd gone through, that wonderful, kind young man she'd once met on a summer day. Her love spilled over, gilding the memory of those long-ago days when they'd both been so young.

"I've led a rough life at times—brawls and women and drinks going down like water. I didn't like that life, so I quit. But I've been a loner for years. You'll have to teach me to share life again. Tell me when I fail—"

She laid her fingers over his lips. "You won't. Welcome home, Wayne Kincaid. Welcome home, my darling."

Rising, she wrapped her arms around him and urged him to her, taking his warmth inside her, savoring the wondrous merging of their bodies and knowing it was also a merging of their souls.

Fourteen

Carey paused outside the door. She'd seen Sophie's head at the window, watching for her, when she arrived. Inside, she could hear her daughter's suppressed giggles. She had a feeling there was a surprise in the making.

She opened the door. The kitchen was empty.

"I'm home," she called as she usually did. She laid her purse on the counter and hung her ratty old cardigan on the peg. Hmm, perhaps she'd better stop at the Army-Navy Store and see about a new one one of these days. "Is anyone here?" she yelled. "Or do I have to eat whatever smells so good all by myself?"

A muffled giggle led her into the living room.

"Surprise," a whole chorus of voices yelled.

Carey really did blink in surprise then. Her living

room was filled with people—moms and dads and kids, some of whom she'd delivered. She stood there with her mouth agape.

"But there are no cars," she protested.

"Happy birthday to you," they all sang.

A cake held pride of place on the coffee table.

She looked at her friends, happiness like a shining bubble inside her. Susan and Ken, Annie and her husband, Bennie, and most of the nurses from the pediatric wing were there. The sheriff and his wife, their two children. Sterling and Jessica and five-year-old Jennifer. Clint and Dakota. Reed Austin and his bride, Janie Carson. Sam Brightwater and his wife and son. Kane and Moriah. Lorrie and Reynaldo. Her own family, Wayne and Sophie, who was a nearly grown-up seven-year-old. And…

"Mom. Dad." She gave each of them a bear hug. "I can't believe you're here."

"Wayne said it was a command performance," her mom explained. "Dad gave up his place in a golf tournament."

"Wow, I'm impressed," she said, teasing her father, who had become obsessed with the game during his retirement.

"Sit," Wayne ordered.

She was treated royally, not standing once as the evening progressed from pinwheels of smoked ham, cheese, tomatoes, avocado, cucumber and lettuce rolled up in flour tortillas and cut into slices; chips; veggies with exotic dips; right to the cake and punch and coffee.

With youngsters in tow, the party broke up early. She was shooed into the bedroom to slip into "something comfortable," her husband suggested with a wicked gleam in his eye. Her parents bundled Sophie up and took her to a cabin they'd rented on the lake for the weekend.

Carey returned to the living room. A fire burned in the grate, although it was late April. She settled on the sofa.

"Here we go," Wayne said, returning to the room with a bundle in his arms. He gave the baby to her.

She smiled into the incredibly blue eyes of Wayne Kincaid III, named after his great-grandfather and father, and opened her gown. The four-month-old latched on and sucked hungrily. The odd sensation of her milk coming down brought a sigh of contentment from her.

Wayne touched her cheek. "Have I told you how very beautiful you are?"

"You might have mentioned it."

Only about once a day, she thought happily. She pressed his hand between her cheek and her shoulder as she cupped their son into the curve of her arm. She suddenly remembered something.

"Winona Cobb once told me, before we were married, that I would receive a Christmas present. My heart's desire, she called it. I didn't pay much attention, but she was right. Our son was born on Christmas Day." She gazed in adoration at the man who took his place beside her on the sofa. "And I do indeed have all my heart's desires. Every one of them."

He settled an arm around her shoulders. "As have I.

Sometimes I remember that I very nearly didn't stop here." He kissed her temple. "I wouldn't have missed loving you for the world."

"We would have met," she declared firmly. "It was fated. Just as you were fated to leave, then return years later when you were needed. Sterling and Clint are very pleased with your management of the resort. Will we be ready for the first guests this summer?"

"Yes. Little more than a month away. June is sparse, July a bit more rushed, then in August—the deluge."

She laughed at his wry note. Studying him covertly, she thought he looked younger and more handsome than ever. He was forty-five now. The gray was gaining on the light and dark strands of blond.

But someplace in her heart, he would always be the handsome young man who had knocked her ice-cream cone into the dirt and bought her another. She closed her eyes and envisioned him as he'd been on that afternoon—beautiful and perfect, her golden idol.

On that day, she'd vowed to marry him. It had taken twenty-five years, but she'd done it. Her hero had come home to her after all.

* * * * *

HARLEQUIN®

INTRIGUE

WILL THIS REUNITED FAMILY
BE STRONG ENOUGH TO EXPOSE
A LURKING KILLER?

FIND OUT IN THIS ALL-NEW
THRILLING TRILOGY FROM TOP
HARLEQUIN INTRIGUE AUTHOR

B.J. DANIELS

WHITEHORSE
MONTANA

Winchester Ranch

GUN-SHY BRIDE—*April 2010*

HITCHED—*May 2010*

TWELVE-GAUGE GUARDIAN—
June 2010

ROMANCE, RIVALRY
AND A FAMILY REUNITED

THE BRIDES
of
BELLA ROSA

William Valentine and his beloved wife, Lucia, live
a beautiful life together, but when his former love Rosa
and the secret family they had together resurface,
an instant rivalry is formed. Can these families
get through the past and come together as one?

Step into the world of Bella Rosa
beginning this April with

Beauty and the Reclusive Prince
by

RAYE MORGAN

Eight volumes to collect and treasure!

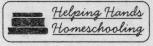

Single father Ian Ferguson's daughter is finally coming out of her shell thanks to the twenty-three-year-old tutor Alexa Michaels. Although Alexa is young—and too pretty—she graduated from the school of hard knocks and is challenging some of Ian's old-school ways. Could this dad learn some valuable lessons about love, family and faith from the least likely teacher?

Look for

Love Lessons

by

Margaret Daley

Helping Hands
Homeschooling

Available April
wherever books are sold.

www.SteepleHill.com

Steeple
Hill®

LI87590

HARLEQUIN *Presents*

2 Stories in 1

HER MEDITERRANEAN PLAYBOY

Sexy and dangerous—he wants you in his bed!

The sky is blue, the azure sea is crashing
against the golden sand and the sun is hot.

The conditions are perfect for
a scorching Mediterranean seduction
from two irresistible untamed playboys!

Indulge your senses with these two delicious stories

A MISTRESS AT THE ITALIAN'S COMMAND
by Melanie Milburne

ITALIAN BOSS, HOUSEKEEPER MISTRESS
by Kate Hewitt

Available April 2010 from Harlequin Presents!

www.eHarlequin.com

HP12910

REQUEST YOUR FREE BOOKS!

2 FREE NOVELS PLUS 2 FREE GIFTS!

SPECIAL EDITION
Life, Love and Family!

YES! Please send me 2 FREE Silhouette® Special Edition® novels and my 2 FREE gifts (gifts are worth about $10). After receiving them, if I don't wish to receive any more books, I can return the shipping statement marked "cancel." If I don't cancel, I will receive 6 brand-new novels every month and be billed just $4.24 per book in the U.S. or $4.99 per book in Canada. That's a saving of 15% off the cover price! It's quite a bargain! Shipping and handling is just 50¢ per book in the U.S. and 75¢ per book in Canada.* I understand that accepting the 2 free books and gifts places me under no obligation to buy anything. I can always return a shipment and cancel at any time. Even if I never buy another book from Silhouette, the two free books and gifts are mine to keep forever.

235 SDN E4NC   335 SDN E4NN

Name	(PLEASE PRINT)	
Address		Apt. #
City	State/Prov.	Zip/Postal Code

Signature (if under 18, a parent or guardian must sign)

Mail to the **Silhouette Reader Service:**
IN U.S.A.: P.O. Box 1867, Buffalo, NY 14240-1867
IN CANADA: P.O. Box 609, Fort Erie, Ontario L2A 5X3

Not valid for current subscribers to Silhouette Special Edition books.

Want to try two free books from another line?
Call 1-800-873-8635 or visit www.morefreebooks.com.

* Terms and prices subject to change without notice. Prices do not include applicable taxes. N.Y. residents add applicable sales tax. Canadian residents will be charged applicable provincial taxes and GST. Offer not valid in Quebec. This offer is limited to one order per household. All orders subject to approval. Credit or debit balances in a customer's account(s) may be offset by any other outstanding balance owed by or to the customer. Please allow 4 to 6 weeks for delivery. Offer available while quantities last.

Your Privacy: Silhouette is committed to protecting your privacy. Our Privacy Policy is available online at www.eHarlequin.com or upon request from the Reader Service. From time to time we make our lists of customers available to reputable third parties who may have a product or service of interest to you. If you would prefer we not share your name and address, please check here. ☐

Help us get it right—We strive for accurate, respectful and relevant communications. To clarify or modify your communication preferences, visit us at www.ReaderService.com/consumerschoice.

SSE10